THE CHATTERTOOTH ELEVEN
EDUARD BASS

**A Tale of a Czech Football Team
for Boys Old and Young**

The Chattertooth
Eleven

Eduard Bass

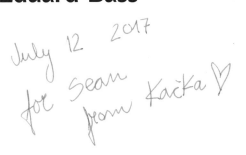

July 12 2017
for Sean
from Kačka ♡

Charles University in Prague
Karolinum Press 2009

ISBN 978-80-246-1573-8

From the moment it was published, in 1922, Klapzubova jedenáctka (The Chattertooth Eleven) was a huge success, running through over thirty editions. It was made into a film directed by Ladislav Brom as early as 1938. Seventy years on it continues to be very popular. It is no surprise that Divadlo Minor, *a famous theatre in Prague, as recently as 2005 decided to bring the book to the stage in a production directed by Petr Forman, son of the famous film director Miloš Forman.* Divadlo Minor *traditionally focused on children, but in the last few years it has sought to draw in adults as well and produce plays for the whole family. What could be more appropriate than the story of Klapzuba (Chattertooth) and his eleven sons, sub-titled 'a tale of a Czech football team for boys young and old'? Indeed the book has always been a great favourite among young and older readers alike – which in modern parlance would mean it has that crossover potential, something publishers are always looking for.*

The Chattertooth Eleven take on all comers and defeat them, first at home and then abroad. In order to do so they have to do much more than show footballing talent. With one side they have to come out onto the pitch looking like Michelin Men with huge leg-pads, because the strategy of their opponents

(Barcelona, as it happens) is to commit enough fouls to disable them. In fact the Chattertooth Eleven scrupulously maintain fair play during their time at the top, breaking with tradition only when faced with cannibals as opposition ('Cheating is cheating and the world's a dirty place. But with God's help we shall escape the frying-pan'). Bar the need to escape the bubbling pot, the Chattertooth team believes in working hard, fair play, mucking in and being true to one another. If the Crown Prince of Brazil (the King of England becomes the Emperor of Brazil in the translation, perhaps for reasons of wartime delicacy) wants to play with them, then he has to sweat for it like anyone else (besides, 'the best King is the one who has the fewest servants'). The team must never become too mechanical, losing their flair. They should never forget that football is a game, not a life (a boy from a village team who refuses to play against them declares 'we play for honour. You play for money'). They are warned of the dangers of complacency. And as for girls, in the face of whose charms 'some kind of peculiar magic seemed to have enveloped the young people,' they should be careful not to fall for the ones who are only out to enjoy a vicarious fame.

The author, Eduard Bass, was born in Prague in 1888 and died in 1946, living through Nazi occupation and surviving it by just nine months. His versatile career included working as a journalist, editor and cabaret director as well as a writer. It is no surprise that his most famous work, apart from Klapzubova jedenátcka, *was* Cirkus Humberto *(1941), about the life of a circus troupe. Bass was well-known for being good company, but humour travels through languages with more difficulty than anything else. Only if you know that in Czech restaurants people order not a 'small' or 'large' wine but 'one tenth' or 'two tenths' (jedno deci/dvě deci) of a litre, does it make sense that Bass asked for a large wine (two tenths) because 'one might feel lonely and abandoned'.*

This translation by Ruby Hobling is very much a product of its period (it was published in 1943, with drawings by Joseph Čapek), but that is one of its delights. It is perfectly readable – indeed like all the best translations it doesn't read like one. Its vocabulary might be uncommon (boys do not now fall out 'on account of a petticoat') but it is certainly not unrecognisable. In the first few pages we read that when the boys have to think brains are racked rather than loaves used, while they 'raise Cain' when they complain. The lankiest is a 'maypole of a lad', their trainer looks 'as if he didn't know how many beans make two' and their first opponents have 'a high-falutin name'. When they get over-excited there is a 'general scrimmage' (very St. Trinian's). All these expressions are used in contemporary English, but taken together they convey an atmosphere and reveal a style of mid-twentieth century comic writing. One can imagine P. G. Wodehouse's Gussy Finknottle having problems knowing how many beans make two, while Bertie would be highly wary of anyone with a high-falutin name in the Drones club. On the other hand he would love a spot of fresh country air around Nether Buckwheat, the beautifully chosen name of the village from which the Chattertooth Eleven come ('Lower' Buckwheat would have been quite wrong as a translation of 'Dolni': think Nether as in 'Netherlands'). Readers will enjoy the wonderful line when the boys are hauled before the inhabitants of Cannibal Island and find themselves facing 'a circle of pedestalled gods with mouths agape,' not to mention the monosyllabic conversation on board ship that cements a lifelong friendship between Old Chattertooth and an Anglo-Indian colonel.

It is difficult to discover very much about the life of Ruby Hobling, but we know that she graduated from Somerville College, Oxford and then went on to teach English at a school in London. She turns up again teaching in Poland and she may well have spoken Polish, Czech and German, moving between the various parts of Central Europe in a way that was possible in the 1920s and early 1930s and only again in the 1990s after both fascism and communism had finally been cleared away.

We also know that she translated at least one other book, whose authors were also part of a complicated Central European mix. In 1947 Nicholson and Watson published a book called Warrior of God *on the great mediaeval Czech reformer Jan (John) Hus, who was burnt at the stake in 1415. In the authors' note Paul Roubiczek (who later went on to be a very well-known philosopher of existentialism) and Joseph Kalmer explain that they left Czechoslovakia just before the outbreak of war and that all their notes were lost in transit. Kalmer had left Austria for Czechoslovakia in 1938 after the 'Anschluss' with Austria. Now the occupation of Bohemia was forcing him to leave again. The two of them went to London, but all they could take with them was the manuscript. They therefore apologise for the absence of a bibliography while they thank Ruby Hobling 'for her invaluable help and inexhaustible patience in the translation of this book'. It is history written with fervour – 'Hus had looked death in the face; the flames could not frighten him even though they were already consuming his books.' Doubtless there was something in the story of the martyr that could have strengthened the resolve of a Chattertooth, and that in turn may be part of the reason why this book was chosen to be published in wartime London by 'The Czechoslovak', based in Fursecroft in London's George Street. The name still remains but as a block* of flats; during the war it was used for several ministries including the Czechoslovak Research Institute and was one of the places used by the Czech government-in-exile.

Old Chattertooth laments the fact that nations don't produce football teams instead of armies, 'I wish to God as it were so, and then Bohemia would be a great power'. When this book was translated into English Bohemia was busy simply surviving, but the rules of life (and, if you ignore the offside rule, the rules of football) have remained much the same in the sixty-five years since. No one will find it hard to enjoy this in the twenty-first century as a tale for all time, even though Planička of Slavia has now become Čech of Chelsea.

Brussels, May 2008   Mark Corner

I.　　In Nether Buckwheat, in the province of Bohemia in Czechoslovakia, there once lived a poor cottager named Chattertooth. He had eleven sons and not a penny in his pocket. He used to rack his brains as to what to put his sons to. At last he decided to make a football team of them.

Behind the cottage was a level piece of meadow; this he called the Playing Field. Then he sold the

goat, bought two balls with the money, and set about training the boys. Honza, the eldest, was a maypole of a lad, so he was put in goal: and as the two youngest, Frantik and Jura, were small and wiry, old Chatter-tooth put them at outside right and left.

He would wake the boys at five in the morning and walk them briskly through the woods for an hour. As soon as they had covered four miles the order would be given, "About turn and back at the double." Only after that did the boys get their breakfast, and then work began in real earnest. And old Chattertooth saw to it that everyone of them knew his job inside out. He taught them how to take a ball in mid-air, stop it and pass, to feint, to centre, to kick from a stationary position or on the run, to throw the ball in, and indeed everything that a footballer should know.

That in itself was a good deal, but it was not by a long chalk all that the Chattertooth boys had to learn. There was running and jumping as well; they had to cover anything from a hundred yards to five miles, and they soon became as good at pole-jumping and at the hop, step and jump as at high and long jumping: and of course they had to know all about hurdle racing as well, and how to set off to a good start.

But even all this did not satisfy old Chattertooth. When the boys had learnt to put the weight and throw the javelin and discus to develop their arm muscles, they had to learn classical wrestling to keep their whole bodies in trim.

Before all else, however, they did breathing exercises with light dumb-bells, for old Chattertooth always said that without good lungs and a good heart training of any kind was nothing but murder and sudden death. In a word, they were kept so busy that they stormed the kitchen like hungry wolves at midday, gobbled up their food, and left their plates looking as if a cat had licked them. Then for an hour they lay down in a row, either on the floor of the cottage or on the bare earth of the yard outside, and rested. Hardly a word was exchanged, for each was glad to be able to stretch his bones and do nothing for a while. As soon as the hour was up old Chattertooth put aside his pipe, drew out his whistle and blew it to assemble the lads, and then the fun started again. Towards evening the old man put on his football boots and joined the boys in a six-a-side game. At the end of the day they streamed back into the house, and old Chattertooth massaged them in turn and threw three pails of cold water over each, as there was no shower-bath in the cottage. This was followed by a light evening meal. For a while they talked to each other, but soon they were sent to bed. Next morning the same old round started anew.

Day in, day out, this went on for three years. At the end of the third year Father Chattertooth popped along to Prague and came back with a sign-board which he nailed on to the gate of the field. It had a blue border, and on a white background was painted in red letters:

THE CHATTERTOOTH ELEVEN

In his pocket he had a paper stating that the Chattertooth Eleven had been enrolled in the third division of the Central Bohemian Football League.

The boys all raised Cain because they were only in the third division, but old Chattertooth said tranquilly: "Everything in its turn. With God's help you will one day beat the Slavia Club and be top of the League, but you must work your way up to that. I have taught you all you need, but getting to the top depends on you yourselves. That is the way of the world."

For a while the boys went on grumbling, but bedtime came and they all fell asleep except Frantik and Jura, who kept on whispering to each other for a long time before they could agree just how they would get one goal after another against Planička of the Slavia Club of Prague, a remarkably fine goalkeeper.

In the spring the League matches started. The Chattertooths went to Prague. They were to make their first appearance against the Hlubočepy Football and Athletic Club. Nobody had ever heard of the Chattertooth Eleven, and the crowd made jokes about the name and grinned from ear to ear at the appearance of the eleven shy village lads who had never seen a town before. They had lambskin caps on their heads, and as for their trainer, well, this old country fellow with his pipe in the corner of his mouth looked as if he didn't know how many beans made two.

From the moment the whistle blew, however, the Chatter-tooths piled on the goals, and at half-time led 39–0. That proved too much for the team with the high-falutin name, and they did not appear after the interval. They explained that the League Committee had made a mistake, and that the opposing team certainly did not belong to the third division. Old Chattertooth sat there, with an ear cocked first in this direction and then in that, so that not a word escaped him of what the people around him were saying. He smiled to himself in silent amusement, chuckled and shifted his pipe from one corner of his mouth to the other, and his eyes shone like a tomcat's. Finally, when he heard the referee say that there had been some mistake which he would report to the provincial committee, he fetched the boys from the pavilion, patted them approvingly on the back, one by one, and led them off home.

On Wednesday the postman turned up with a fat letter. The letter said that by a decision of the provincial committee the Chattertooth Eleven had been promoted to the second division and was to play the Vršovice Sports Club on the following Sunday. Old Chattertooth chuckled quietly, and the boys gurgled with laughter.

Sunday found them in Vršovice. Thousands of people had collected there, for the news had spread from Prague of what a remarkable team these Chat-

tertooths were. The old man, with the inevitable pipe in his mouth, once more sat there blinking at the boys as they won 14-0. Once again there was a babel of protests, and once more a fat letter turned up – the Chattertooth Eleven was in the first division.

Now it was no longer possible to jump up into a higher division. And so they just had to go on beating one club after another: the Headers Sports Club 13-0, the Neck-or-Nothing Athletic Club 16-0, the Cokernut Club 12-0, the Kladno Spartans 11-0, the Czech Karlin 9-0, the Meteors of Prague VIII 10-0, the C.A.F.C. 8-0, the Plzeň Sports Club 15-0, the Teplice Athletic Football Club 7-0, and the Victoria 6-0.

In the semi-finals they found themselves up against the famous Sparta Eleven. For a week beforehand old Chattertooth put them into light training, massaged them thoroughly, and on Sunday, just before the match, he reshuffled his team. Two hours later he sent his wife a telegram:

SPARTA BEATEN SIX NIL STOP HONZA FELL ASLEEP IN GOAL WITH BOREDOM STOP CHATTERTOOTH.

On the same Sunday the Slavia Club beat the Union Club 3-2.

A week later the Chattertooth Eleven met the victorious club. There was such a crowd in the Stadium that the soldiers had to be called out to close all the roads leading to it. Any other matches arranged for the day were cancelled so that everyone could watch the Chattertooth Eleven.

The boys came by omnibus from Nether Buckwheat to the Stadium. Old Chattertooth sat beside the driver and watched the crowd. He led his sons into the dressing-room and stayed with them until they were in their football costume. Then he said:

"Well, boys, are you going to show 'em what you can do?"

"Of course," they answered.

Two of the committee came and led the father to the seats ot honour, where they placed him next to the Mayor of Prague, the Chief of the Police, and the Minister of Finance. Smoking was forbidden there, but when old Chattertooth took out his pipe the Chief of Police gave a sign to the man on duty not to stop him.

When the Chattertooth Eleven appeared there was sudden confusion as sixty photographers charged on to the field to take photographs of the miracle team. At last order was restored and the referee blew his whistle.

The Chattertooth boys were at the top of their form. The Slavia team, too, played a good game, but at half-time the score was 3–0 for the Chattertooth Eleven. In the second half they got another three, and won easily by 6–0. The boys from Nether Buckwheat were borne back in triumph to their hotel by the crowd, shoulder high. Before the hotel there was such a crowd that the Chief of the Police had to beg Mr. Chattertooth to address them; otherwise they would have refused to budge. So old Chattertooth went out on to the balcony, took his pipe from his mouth, pushed his lambskin cap on the back of his head, and, once the wildly cheering crowd below him had calmed down, began:

"Well, it's like this. I just said to them, well, boys, I said, you just learn 'em. And they did learn 'em. There's nothing like children doing what they're told by their parents."

And that was the speech made by old Chattertooth to twenty thousand people when his team had won the championship with a total score of 122–0.

II.   Long before the boys had won the Final the foreign newspapers were full of tales about the Chattertooth Eleven. The leading European sports papers sent reporters to Prague to take a look at these wizards of the soccer pitch. All kinds of strange gentlemen in hairy tweeds and check caps turned up one after another at the poor little cottage in Nether Buckwheat to make offers of matches abroad to old Chattertooth. Father Chattertooth listened attentively, took his calendar out of the table drawer, made a note of what each gentleman promised, and then pored over his notes for many an hour. The boys knew that their father was hatching out some scheme or other for them, but until

they had won the championship they did not bother him with questions.

Once the famous match against Slavia had been won they bought all the newspapers, which were full of long articles about themselves, complete with photographs, and took them home to their mother. She, poor simpleton, began to cry because her sons were so famous and respected. She thanked God that the whole business was now done with.

"What are you chattering about, Mařenka?" asked old Chattertooth.

"Well, as long as they were only novices," said Mrs. Chattertooth, "I was always feeling sorry for them. They had such a hard time of it. But now they are masters of their job and can take it easy for a bit. Like old Kopejtko, our neighbour. He had to work like a horse at first, too – but he's got on, and now he is boss and can hire other people to do the work for him."

"Goodness gracious me, Mařenka," said old Chattertooth, shaking his head with annoyance, "you women will never in all your lives learn the first thing about sport. Do you mean to say that you think we are going to hire eleven men to play for us while we look on?"

"Naturally that would be the best thing to do."

"Well, in all my born days I must say I have never been able to guess what you women will think of next. Why, our real troubles are only just beginning... Come here, boys."

And Chattertooth took his notebook out of the drawer, knocked out his pipe, put his spectacles on his nose to make sure that the boys were all there, and then started:

"Now we are all quietly here together just take a look at Jura's nose."

They all turned and stared at Jura, who went bright red.

But there was nothing special to be learnt from his nose.

"Look hard," their father urged, "and see how he is sticking it in the air just because he shot three goals against Slavia. As if you could rest on your laurels after a victory in Bohemia. You are the champions in the first division. Good. You are the best team in the country. Very good. And is that going to satisfy you? Do you think you can live on the memory of that until your dying day? Well, you are wrong, I think. People must always keep on trying for something more, something that is just beyond their reach. If you are champions at home, then you have got to aim at being champions of the world. And you must not give up trying as long as there is still something lacking and you are short of your goal. At the moment almost everything is lacking. You will soon stop giving yourself airs when you meet a team that beats you 7-0 and licks you into a cocked hat. Now I have been talking the matter over with a number of fine gentlemen, and I have decided that – well, that we will look around Europe a little. I have made a list of the places we'll go to. First Berlin, and then Hamburg, Copenhagen, Oslo, Stockholm, Warsaw, Budapest, Vienna, Zurich, Milan, Marseilles, Barcelona, Lyons, Paris, Brussels, Amsterdam, and London. When you've won all those matches you can stick up your noses as high as heaven as far as I am concerned. But until then don't get swelled heads. And now see to your packing.

The day after tomorrow we are off to Germany."

The boys had listened attentively, but the moment he finished they sprang up, howled with excitement, and started pitching into each other for sheer joy that they were going to see the world. Then they fetched a map to see where they were going. They nearly kissed their father and mother to death, and Jura even crept into the dog's kennel to tell Nero about their journey. Old Chattertooth had to take a stick to them to get them to bed that night. As soon as the paraffin lamp had been put out and old Chattertooth himself had gone off to bed, Jura sat up, bent over to Frantik, roared "Denmark!" and dug him in the ribs. And Frantik, not to be outdone, cried: "Switzerland!" and tried to throttle his brother. And the others, not slow in following their example, shouted to each other: "Oh Boy! Norway!" "Berlin, you chaps!" "Just think, Paris!" "And what about Spain?" "England!" And all the time the pillows were flying about. There was a general scrimmage until they were all out of breath. Then they sat on the edge of their beds and put their heads together to decide how they would tackle this team and that. They quarrelled so vigorously that they didn't fall asleep till dawn.

The next day everything was turned upside down in the Chattertooth cottage. The boys kept running here and there fetching armfuls of stuff that they thought they might need for the journey. The next minute they would change their minds and go and fetch something else. Everything was topsy-turvy, and not a moment of quiet was known till the evening when the trunks stood ready packed in the corner and the boys sat down to their last supper in Nether Buckwheat.

Mother cried when they took leave of her next morning, and she was indeed unhappy as she pottered around the cottage. Nero alone remained with her. He stuck to her like a shadow. Only when he itched specially hard did he sit down to scratch himself, and even then he followed Mrs. Chattertooth around with his eyes.

A week passed. Then came the postman with a telegram. The Chattertooth Eleven had won twelve to nought in Berlin, and all were in good health. "Thank Heaven," Mrs. Chattertooth sighed with relief. "I know I am behind the times, but if it weren't for that nought I don't know what mischief Father might not be up to."

And then came one telegram after another, one newspaper after another, one letter after another. They all spoke of victories and noughts. The Chattertooths had swept across Europe from north to south. After beating Milan 6–0 they set out once more on their journey, this time to meet the Spaniards.

The Chattertooths were no longer the gaping, self-conscious village boys who had taken the field in Prague. They had seen something of the world and had the corners rubbed off them. They wore American suits, square-toed shoes, and tweed caps. There were no flies on them now. Only old Chattertooth had not changed in the least.

"If people need me they will take me as I am," he said to the boys when they tried to persuade him to dress fashionably.

"I shall stick to the clothes I have grown old in."

And he pushed his lambskin cap on the back of his head, took out his old pipe with the huntsman painted on it, filled it, and then with every draw filled the first-class railway carriage with such a smell that he and his sons were always left to themselves. Nobody else could stand old Chattertooth's strong shag.

III.   Not merely the whole of Barcelona but half Spain was agog with excitement. On all sides you could see placards with "Checco-Eslovaquia" printed on them in huge letters. This was what the Spanish made of the name Czechoslovakia. There was one subject on everybody's tongue – what would be the result of the match between the champions of Catalonia and the mysterious Chattertooth team, about which the most extraordinary stories were appearing in all the newspapers in the world. Even if three-quarters of these stories were rubbish, one fact remained unchallenged – the total result of the Chattertooth matches, which always showed a nought on the one side and on the other a figure that began to look more and more like the date of the current year rather than a football score. The

Barcelona Football Club felt that its whole reputation was at stake. Several meetings of the team and of the Club Committee were held in order to decide how these foreigners should be tackled. The meetings were excited and stormy, but finally Alcantara's opinion began to prevail.

"Gentlemen! You are naturally at liberty to have your own opinions on the matter," he said at one meeting, "but I think it would be best to knock out these Chattertooths at the start, before they get into their stride. Safety first, you know. I have never known a centre-forward with a broken rib save the situation."

"Hear, hear," cried the others. "We'll break three of his ribs right at the beginning. You can't be too sure."

"If you take my advice we'll first settle the two insides and the centre-forward. That should be enough for the first half."

"Play for safety and break the collarbone of the goalkeeper as well."

Then someone suggested that it would be a better idea to cripple the two outsides and one of the backs. Another of the Barcelona team was in favour of a central attack, and recommended a tactical combination of the centre-forward, the centre-half, and the goalkeeper. Others had different ideas. If they all had their way the whole Chattertooth Eleven would be in hospital five minutes after the kick-off.

"Splendid!" the players shouted. "And then we'll just go on kicking as many goals as we like."

"Gentlemen," said the president of the club at last, "I am touched beyond words when I see how you vie with one another to secure victory for our colours. But it is not such plain sailing as you seem to think. If you make cold meat of the whole lot you will not be able to score a single goal."

"Why not? What do you mean? You just wait and see!" roared the team.

"Gentlemen, I am afraid there is nothing to be done about it. We should not be able to shoot one goal against the Chattertooths."

"And why not?"

"Because we should all be off-side the whole time."

The players gasped dispiritedly at each other and were silent. It was indeed plain that they would be off-side if nobody was facing them.

The President, taking advantage of their surprise, continued:

"And so I think that we should not overdo the business. I think Alcantara's suggestion is enough for a start. Cripple the insides and the centre-forward to begin with and then see how things are going. If that turns out to be insufficient, I will whistle the first few bars of our national anthem, and that will be the sign for you to lay out the two wingers and one of the backs. And if that is still not enough, we shall act on the third proposal and put the centre line out of action. But for heaven's sake leave at least three men intact against us or we shall be off-side."

This proposal was accepted unanimously, and they all went home feeling that they had victory in their pockets. The next day the whole of Barcelona was full of the news and joy was unbounded. Then the papers published photographs of Josef and Tonik Chattertooth, the two insides, and of Karel, the centre-forward. In column-long articles, history, natural science and mathematics were all ransacked to prove that these Chattertooths were three of the roughest and toughest of customers, and Barcelona must keep an eye on them. The people joked about it in all the barbers' shops, inns, and pastry-cooks', and the apprentices and shop-boys drew crosses under the photographs, as though the three players had already met their fate and their hash was settled "for ever and ever, amen." That was the state of affairs when the Chattertooth Eleven arrived in Barcelona.

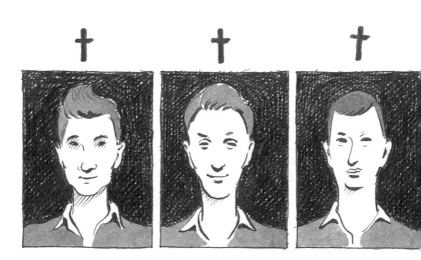

They had still three clear days before the match, and so they strolled about the town staring at anything that happened to interest them. The first thing that they scrambled for each day was the newspapers, and old Chattertooth always made it his job to get them. But whatever paper he happened to open, he found photographs only of Josef, Tonik and Karel. And little crosses were always drawn under them.

"What on earth does this mean?" old Chattertooth kept asking himself in perplexity, and while the boys were wandering about the town he sat in front of his hotel, blew thick clouds of smoke from his pipe, and tried in vain to make head or tail of the seemingly double-Dutch captions under the photographs. These three crosses that turned up everywhere became a nightmare to him. He vowed that as soon as they returned home the lads should learn foreign languages so that they should not be at everybody's mercy as he was.

Sunday came. The match was at five o'clock in the afternoon, but by midday people had already begun streaming towards the football ground. People hurried towards the entrances in crowds, taking no notice of the outlandish old man who sat on a stone by the wayside, a lambskin cap on his head in spite of the heat of the Spanish sun, smoking his pipe as he watched the hurrying throng. Never had old Chattertooth been so worried as he was that day. He scented something hostile and treacherous in the wind, but could not get to the bottom of it. The boys had no cares: life was easy enough for them: but he was on tenterhooks. He had locked the boys into a room in the hotel to keep them out of harm's way and then gone out to stretch his legs a little and look around. These three crosses haunted him, but still he could find no explanation for them.

As he sat there by the curb he suddenly heard shouts and a honking of cars. People sprang to one side and crowded onto the pavement to make way for three Red Cross ambulances which came down the street. Old Chattertooth looked at the cars, looked at the red crosses on them, counted one, two, three, pushed his cap back, scratched himself behind one ear, and saw the cars disappear into the football ground. Then he took his pipe from between his teeth, spat and growled:

"You hellhounds, you sons of Satan, so you want..."

And then he shut his eyes and hissed through his teeth into his beard; "Naturally that would be just the sort of thing a lot of dirty vagabonds like you would do. To think that I should only just have tumbled to it, you..."

He untwisted the stem of his pipe, knocked out the ashes, refilled his pipe, and hastened back to the hotel at top speed.

It was just two o'clock. The omnibus that would take them to the ground would leave at four.

Never before had the boys taken any luggage with them to the field, but this time old Chattertooth dragged down the hotel steps a huge wicker basket that he had once bought in Berlin. The boys had no idea what was in the basket. The valet and the porter heaved it onto the roof of the omnibus, the boys climbed in, and the old man, as was his habit, took his seat beside the driver, who pressed his foot on the starter. The omnibus rattled away towards the football field. Old Chattertooth had already recovered from his fright a little, but as he watched the people going to the match, all looking darkly at his boys, he could not restrain himself and muttered and growled the whole way.

The boys had already noticed what a strange mood he was in, but could not explain it. There was something also that puzzled them. What was in that great basket? At the ground it took two men to carry it into the dressing-room. Old Chattertooth meanwhile said not a word but paced up and down, growling softly like a cat playing with a mouse. And when the boys began to change he shut the door and turned the key twice in the lock.

Chattertooth's sons had never taken so long to dress as they did that day. The Barcelona Eleven stood waiting on the field, forty-five thousand people shouted, whistled, and catcalled from their seats, the referee and the linesman wandered about like lost hens, but there was no sign of the Chattertooth team. At last a light brown speck appeared in the black sea of people before the stands, a ball flew high into the air, and the Chattertooth Eleven entered the field.

Forty-five thousand people stood thunderstruck, in silent stupefaction. The next moment a roar of laughter broke out. Since the world and football began, no team had ever appeared on the field dressed like the Chattertooth boys were. Their legs were as thick as tree trunks, and on looking closer you could see that under their stockings they

had bound on huge leg-pads. Around their knees were pneumatic rubber tyres. Their thighs were protected back and front with strong pads of rubber. Their arms above and below the elbow were similarly protected. Each wore a crash helmet on his head, as if he were taking part in a T. T. race. But their bodies were funniest of all.

For the Chattertooths looked like a team of Fat Boys from *Pickwick*.

Yes, these lads, whose lithe and resilient figures were famous throughout the world, looked today like men overburdened with a heavy load of fat. Eleven plump melons had been put on sturdy legs and set in motion, it seemed. The jaws of the Barcelona team dropped. Alcantara sidled up and hit Frantik stealthily on the stern. His hand bounced back with such force that his arm was almost dislocated.

The Chattertooths were wearing rubber suits pumped full of air. It was impossible to lay a finger on them.

Alcantara's nose was quite out of joint with disappointment, and the entire Barcelona team looked crestfallen. The citizens of Barcelona were disconcerted, too; only one person in one of the central grandstands let out one loud laugh. That was old Chattertooth, who drew at his pipe and was so hard put to it to suppress his laughter that the tears rolled down his cheeks. "Murder-plague-and-sudden-death," he swore to himself from time to time, when he was not actively engaged in swallowing back his mirth, "they won't be able to move very quickly, done up like balloons. But what does it matter? You can't risk your life for the sake of a little comfort. If only they remember what I told them."

The boys indeed remembered. They played exactly as he had told them. When they had once secured the ball they passed to each other with the longest shots possible, the left back to the outside right, the right back to the outside left, and the outsides to each other. The rest of them only shared in the game in front of the goal. The result was that the Spaniards charged right or left, but before they had reached the Chattertooth who had the ball at the moment, the ball was already flying back across their heads to the other end of the field where not one of them stood. And before you could say Jack Robinson the ball flew into the net, and again, and a third and a fourth time, in quick succession. In despair the Spaniards tried to cover the wings, but the Chattertooth boys countered these tactics by close passing between the insides. Then every man-jack of the Spanish team threw himself against the Czech attack, but without avail. In short, it was a game in which the Spaniards never got near the Chattertooths, for as soon as they approached the ball was well away somewhere else. They shot into the Spanish goal from such great distances and with such great speed and accuracy that the goalkeeper was just able to turn five shots for corners. Apart from these five, every shot was a goal. In the second half of the game Alcantara ran completely amok and without the slightest reason suddenly kicked Tonik in the breast with both feet. A terrible screech was heard, Alcantara bounced ten yards into the air, and Tonik stood there in the middle of the field, suddenly grown thin, with his dress hanging down round him like a scarecrow.

"That doesn't matter, son," cried the old man from his seat. "I'll blow you up again at once."

He was as good as his word, and in a minute he had mended the puncture and blown the suit up again, and when the sun went down the Chattertooths had won 31 to nil.

"Shabby lot of beggars, these Spaniards," chuckled old Chattertooth, as he helped his sons out of their 'armour.' "They are laughing on the other sides of their faces now, and it serves them right for drawing crosses over my boys' pictures."

The emergency dressing stations had their hands full that day. The ambulances could not cope with all the work and had to send for reinforcements, for during the match – two hundred and seventy-five Spaniards in the stands had literally burst with rage!

IV.   "Oh, Mr. Allenby, just one more thing. What do you think the crowd numbers?"

"Ninety thousand, they said a quarter of an hour ago at the box-office. All records have been broken, Cormick."

"And what are the odds?"

"Three to one on Muddlesfield. We simply must win. England expects, you know..."

"Thanks, Mr. Allenby. Goodbye."

"Goodbye, Cormick. Be seeing you soon."

This conversation took place in the grandstand of the biggest football ground in London. Allenby, a director of the stadium, cordially pressed the hand of Cormick, a reporter on the *New Sporting Life*. Then he sat down once more in his seat as the reporter vanished down the gangway.

It seemed an endless gangway through which thousands of excited people were now streaming. Cormick slipped through the crowd like an eel, cut across to the stairs leading to the public stands, ran up them, and slipped along to the end of the last row. There a little door was cut in the woodwork. Cormick pulled a key out of his pocket, opened the door, and went onto a little balcony built on the outside wall of the stand. Far below him was a big square into which three broad roads led. At the moment a black crowd of people and vehicles made

the square look like a vast ant-hill. All were pressing towards the many entrances to the football field. The air quivered with the excited shouting of innumerable voices and the deafening roar of warning horns from the motor cars. Like three unending snakes the three streets poured forth motor cars, buses and vehicles of all sorts, going towards the field. For a moment Cormick watched this surging crowd swimming before his eyes, and then he shut the door behind him and climbed on to the balustrade of the balcony. A little iron emergency staircase had been fixed to the wall before him: rung by rung Cormick climbed on to the roof of the grandstand. This was a vast, evenly sloping expanse glowing hot in the sunshine, and with a flag-staff fixed to the centre of the higher side. Cormick went up to a seat which had been placed beside the flag-staff. He took up a telephone apparatus that was on the seat and put on the headphones, so that both his ears were covered and the mouthpiece was just opposite his mouth. Two wires, several yards long, led to the flag-staff, which was connected by telephone cable to a distant building. At the other end of the wire, many miles away, was the editorial room of *New Sporting Life,* There at a table sat a young man who, like Cormick, was wearing headphones, but had a typewriter in front of him. A few men were sitting in armchairs scattered around the room. They were eagerly waiting for Cormick's report by telephone. On a second table there lay a pane of glass on which someone was ready to paint the progress of the game. The pane would be displayed in an artificially blacked-out window with a light behind it. Hundreds of people had gathered in front of the offices to watch for the first report.

In the meantime Cormick had taken the chair and pushed it close to the edge of the roof. Two flags were flapping on the mast above him: at the top was the Union Jack and below it a pennant with a blue wedge on a red and white background. In the dizzy depth below him he saw the rich green turf of the magnificent field, with the white lines shining in the sun and the dark masses of people in the grandstands. Between the stands and the football pitch itself there, was a broad track used for athletics. About a hundred policemen stood here motionless, evenly spaced out. To Cormick in his breezy height they looked like particularly thick milestones. At the two goals photographers were either sitting or lying on the ground. Cormick glanced with the eyes of a connoisseur at the whole pageant and found it good. He leant back comfortably in his chair, put his right leg over his left knee, took a pair of binoculars out of his bag, adjusted them carefully so that nothing would escape him, and then began his endless conversation with the mouthpiece.

"Hallo, Atkinson, how is everything? That crackling sound? That's the flags just above me. You'll get used to it in a minute. They are cracking like pistol shots. It's pretty windy up so high. But it's better to be sitting here than in the gruelling heat down below. And nobody can butt in on my 'phoning up here. It was a fine idea... Tell Fred he's lost his bet with me. A quarter of an hour ago they had already sold more than ninety thousand tickets. And people are still lining up to get in. If you hear a terrible row in the next few minutes you can tell the world that the grandstands have collapsed under the terrific pressure of people."

"I am afraid I shall not be able to give a vivid eye-witness account. I shall be pitched down about fifty yards, and the telephone wire is too short for that. You think we might begin? All right. You have already got my introduction. Be so good as to read it back to me to see if it needs changing."

Cormick sat silently in his seat and listened to the tiny voice in the earphones. After a couple of minutes he said:

"That's O. K. It can go as it is. It all looks just as I thought it would. Only put a hundred instead of ninety thousand spectators. They're still pouring in. Hallo, ready? Take down now what I dictate: At ten past three there broke out over the field a storm of applause that seemed as though it would go on for ever, as the eleven heroes of the Muddlesfield team ran out onto the field. Winnipeld, looking very cheerful, is at the head and Tank Clark brings up the rear. It is a pleasure to watch the springy movement of their twenty-two legs and to see the rippling of their muscles under their blue and yel-

51

low striped jerseys. The whole of England roars out never-ending cheers to greet the flower of the nation, assembled here to defend the worldwide fame and glory of British football. There is no one who thinks that the champions of the League will disappoint us. The betting stands three to one on, and those taking on bets against Muddlesfield are either foreigners or people who ... wait a minute. Cross that out and we will make a fresh paragraph of it at the end. Have you taken it out? Hallo! I am continuing my dictation. The champions of Europe are coming out. They, too, are greeted by the public with cheers of appreciation which soon, however, give way to curiosity. So these are the famous warriors sent by the ambitious little Republic in the heart of Europe to win her world-wide fame. What a picturesque scene they make, these brothers who have learnt to develop their natural feeling of kinship into outstanding teamwork and to organise themselves into an entity. At first glance they do not look remarkable. Their slight forms cannot compare with those of the athletes of Muddlesfield. They seem bewildered by the sea of people in the stands.

They make for the centre of the field huddled together as if to give each other courage. Surrey, the referee, approaches them. Captain Winnipeld leaves his men to come and greet the guests... Hallo! Look out. Something new coming. Make a subheading of it: His Imperial Highness the Emperor of Brazil. Did you get that? New paragraph. Take my dictation again: At this moment fresh cheers burst out all round the field. The door to the central seats is opened to admit their Imperial Highnesses the Emperor and Empress of Brazil and the Crown Prince of Brazil, now visiting England. Mr. Allenby greets the exalted guests. The royal pair thank the crowd for their enthusiastic reception. With a friendly gesture the Emperor greets the players. Then their Highnesses sit down to watch the greatest match in English history... Make the words 'greatest match in English history' a subtitle on a new line. Have you done that? I am dictating again now: Muddlesfield win the toss and will be playing with the wind at their backs. Breathless suspense and a silence in which you could hear a pin drop descend upon the audience. New paragraph.

The referee blows his whistle. The time is twenty-one minutes and sixteen seconds past three. The centre-forward of the Chattertooths has passed the ball to the inside right, Charcot runs forward, but the inside right flicks the ball to the right winger. Charcot has overtaken the winger and got the ball. ...Hallo! No, cross that out. The devil alone knows how the boy did it, but he has kept the ball. I am dictating again: Barring and Winnipeld hurry to Charcot's help. A shot – the ball flies across the field to the left wing. A wonderful pass, right between the defence. A lightning rush along the left touchline. Who is the quicker? The little winger of the red and whites has reached the ball. Forward, Warsey! Too late. Centre! Much too high. The ball is going stomach high. The inside left and the centre-forward miss it. Gorringer, the left back is raising his foot. Where did that inside right suddenly appear from? He passes the ball across to the inside left. Warsey! Oh damnation, it's passed him. Jumping Jehoshaphat! Bang! What the devil –! What? of course, it's in the net already. Ye Gods! That was a shot! The public? Dead silent. Now they burst into cheers. That was absolutely shattering. How long did it take? Exactly sixty-seven seconds after the kick-off. Write at that point: A terrific shot by the inside left, such as we have not seen for decades on an English ground. Before Clark could raise his hands the ball was in the net behind him."

Up there on the roof Cormick could scarcely contain his excitement. He stood up and pushed his chair back. Then he began dictating a description of the Muddlesfield attack. He grew lyrical

over the play of his countrymen, but he had to keep on telling Atkinson, the stenographer, to cross out the curses which accompanied his account of the Chattertooth defence. Suddenly he was so completely silent that Atkinson, worried, asked what was wrong. Crestfallen, Cormick answered that the Chattertooths had just scored a second goal.

"It can't be helped: we must admit that the Chattertooths are the better men. Write up in the window that our lads are in good spirits and will turn the tables in the second half. Otherwise you'll have the office stormed. – Hallo! The forty-third minute. From the throw-in we are attacking on the left wing. An exciting struggle is developing in the centre of the field. With long kicks the backs of both sides send the ball to the opposite side of the ground. Charcot darts in and pushes the ball forward. Winnipeld runs up to it, he is alone, and now, now... damn, it's gone over the line. That's what I call bad luck. From the throw-in the ball goes to the right wing – end of the first half. We are losing two-nil. But our men are fresh, and in the second half will get into their stride. The spectators

are glum but admire the perfect game of our opponents. In all conscience, it is no disgrace to be beaten by a team that plays as they do. The Emperor of Brazil is showing clear signs of excitement. The Muddlesfield Committee are explaining to him the reasons why they are two down. Mr. Allenby is leaving them. Now he is returning. A strange-looking old man accompanies him. It is apparently the father of the Chattertooths. I am just going across there to find out what they are saying to each other. Have a breather, Atkinson. I will be back for the beginning of the second half. And make a note please, that the Emperor shook hands with old Chattertooth very heartily."

Cormick threw down the headphones, hurried across the roof, slid down the little ladder, and vanished into the crowd who were busily discussing the first-half play.

V.   Neither the *New Sporting Life* nor any other paper published the conversation that old Chattertooth had with the Emperor of Brazil on that memorable day on which his boys beat the Muddlesfield Football Club four to nil. They printed only a few short passages that were repeated to them by the Muddlesfield Committee. If we are lucky enough to have a much fuller report of that historic talk, it is thanks to the furrier Maceška, one of our countrymen, who acted as interpreter for the Chattertooths in London.

Mr. Vincenc Maceška was a very keen sportsman. True, he did not play football; he did not run or jump either: but that was only, because his eighteen stones handicapped him. He did not practise wrestling either, and he never tried his hand at swimming or rowing. The only sport to which he had ever abandoned himself, but this he did wholeheartedly, was tug-of-war, in which he was the famous "last man". When he had slung the rope round his vast paunch and had dug his short legs well in, so that his body almost touched the ground, the opposing team had all their work cut out to try and shift this mountain of opposing flesh a fraction of an inch. The rest of his team then provided the pull needed for victory. As a result, for eight years nobody could wrest the tug-of-war championship from the Bohemian furrier's team in London; not even the Bear Team of the London police could move a rope with Mr. Vincenc Maceška at its end. Later, Mr. Maceška neglected even this form of exercise, but devoted himself more passionately than ever to sporting activities. There was not a club in his neighbourhood of which he was not president or deputy president, secretary or treasurer. It happened many a time that as secretary of one club he had to challenge himself as president of another. It must be admitted that on such occasions he made use of a rare courtesy of address. The correspondence of some clubs is, alas, marked by a certain sinister acrimony, biting irony, and vitriolic rancour, but the letters written by Mr. Vincenc Maceška of one club to Mr. Vincenc Maceška of another could be printed in any Guide to Letter-writers as examples of a correspondence conducted with an unfailing courtesy of the most exalted type. For every letter, as if written by the hand of a master poet, revealed a lively sense of the personal merits of him to whom the letter was addressed.

The attention of this distinguished devotee of sport was naturally attracted by the arrival of the Chattertooth Eleven. Mr. Vincenc Maceška did not fail to go to Dover to meet his countrymen. And, as the indispensable courier, guide and patron of the Chattertooths, he was invited to receptions two years after the team had left the country.

It is from this famous character that we have the details of the interesting conversation between the Emperor of Brazil and old Chattertooth.

There was a trivial misunderstanding over the first words. The Emperor graciously asked old Chattertooth: "How do you do?" Not waiting for his interpreter, and only grasping the word "How?", Chattertooth immediately answered, "Naturally, Your Imperial Majesty, Mr. Emperor, we give them all a good licking."

Here Mr. Maceška intervened to explain.

"His Majesty doesn't want to know whom you beat, but is asking about your health."

"Oh, gracious goodness, Your Imperial Majesty, Mr. Emperor, what can be the lot of a poor cottager? If it weren't for my boys it might just as well be nil to nil, and if there happened by any chance to be a goal, as like as not it would be offside."

Mr. Maceška grew red in the face and wiped the sweat from his forehead as he considered how these words could be rendered in a manner fit for the ears of the Emperor. But the presence of so much royalty had so confused him that his mind remained a blank, and he stuttered out in English just what old Chattertooth had said in homely Czech. The Emperor smiled and said: "And how is Mrs. Chattertooth? Has she accompanied you on your travels?"

"God forbid, Mr. Emperor. A game of football is not as simple as ruling a country; you can't let the women-folk start having a say in it. Your Majesty must not take my words ill, but a decent game of football, that calls for much more than just ruling an empire."

"So, dear Chattertooth, your opinion of emperors is not very high?"

"Well, I wouldn't go so far as to say that, Your Majesty, Mr. Emperor. Our Lord above has made a host of trades and professions for men to turn their hands to, and why shouldn't there be as good a fellow as another among the crowned heads occasionally? Far be it from me to hurt anybody's feelings. But a trade like your imperial ruling, I'd as soon die like a dog as take it up. The whole business seems to me to be like this. My great grandfather, dead this many a year, may he rest in peace, was with the soldiers in Plzeň, and he told me that in olden times every man there had the right to brew beer. The right remained with the house, even when the owner no longer brewed at home but had set up a brewery somewhere else. And a house may have tumbled down or gone to rack and ruin, but if so much as a doorpost remains, the owner still has the right to brew beer, down to this very day. He may not be able to tell hops from malt if his life depended on it, but he still has the right, and can still make a pretty penny from it, simply because he has inherited a doorpost. And it is much about the same with emperors. Others must do the brewing for them, but they make the money and have the right just because they have inherited a doorpost somewhere or other."

"And so, dear Chattertooth, you have no opinion at all of emperors?"

"Now why not, Your Majesty, Mr. Emperor? As the nation makes its bed, so must it lie in it. There are nags that are happiest when they need not wear harness, and there are others who can't trot a yard till they have their blinkers on. But in the long run the one has to pull loads like the other. There's no way out. And I will say that football playing is much more difficult work than your royal ruling. Just think for a moment what it would be like, Mr. Emperor, if you were standing before the enemy goal and the outside put through a beautiful pass. There stands the Emperor, there is the ball, there is the goal – and you have to call a cabinet meeting first of all to talk the matter over and decide whether it would be better to shoot with the toe or the instep, and whether to shoot into the top right-hand corner or the bottom left-hand corner. Lord have mercy, we should find ourselves lagging pretty far behind when it came to the final score, if we did the likes."

As Mr. Maceška interpreted this more or less literally the Emperor could no longer suppress his laughter.

"You are a cunning old scoundrel, Mr. Chattertooth," he said at last. (At least that was how Mr. Maceška interpreted it.) "I should like to make you a privy councillor."

"There's still time for many things to happen, Your Majesty, Mr. Emperor," laughed old Chattertooth. "If your Highness ever finds himself in a tight corner, just come along to us at Nether Buckwheat. I shall find some way or other of getting you out."

"Joking apart, Mr. Chattertooth, I enjoy speaking to people like you. You have such sound common sense."

"Right as usual, Mr. Emperor," Chattertooth assured him. "The cares that press upon us in our exalted profession are by no means light. How often have I thought, for example, watching a match like today's, how strange it is that football has not been officially proclaimed the measure of a nation's sound mental and physical strength. It demands so much self-control, such an abundance of ideas, wisdom, comradeship and self-sacrifice, in short, so much individual work for the good of the whole, that football, of all sports, best reflects the high development of a social system."

"Why does not each nation try to produce an outstanding football team instead of equipping vast armies? And then if a quarrel developed that could not be settled by peaceful means, instead of armies let each of the quarrelling nations put a football team into the field to decide the thorny question."

"I wish to goodness it were so, and then Bohemia would be a great power," old Chattertooth acquiesced cheerfully.

"Now tell me, Mr. Chattertooth, wouldn't that be better?"

"Your Majesty, Mr. Emperor, wouldn't the Chattertooths be fine allies to have?"

"Think for a moment what difficulties your country has with Hungary, for example. Now how would it be if you and your sons defended your fatherland on the football field?"

"Beg to report, Your Highness, 132 to nil. And perhaps still more, confounded rogues."

"So you see, Mr. Chattertooth, you are a born Minister of War."

"As long as they only shoot goals. But anything more – God forbid. I would rather remain a sergeant with the Chattertooth Eleven."

"Hm. Now tell me, Mr. Chattertooth, did you yourself train your boys?"

"Single-handed, Your Majesty, Mr. Emperor. And if they manage to put up a good show today, it is because blood will tell, and you don't get grapes from thistles."

"We have a special reason for being interested in this. When news of your team was first published in the papers, and ever-fresh tales followed, we one day found our son, the Crown Prince, deep in thought. We asked him what was the matter, and he said: 'Royal Father, why have I not ten brothers, so that we could form a football team like the Chattertooths?' We are deeply attached to our son, the Crown Prince, and try to fulfil his every wish. We therefore betook ourselves to the Apartments of Her Majesty the Empress, and after much discussion came to the conclusion that our son's wishes could hardly be met. But the idea has just come to me that you might take the Crown Prince into your team."

Old Chattertooth quickly raised his head and looked the Emperor straight in the eye.

"Your Majesty, let us put on one side the question of the honour. That would be equally great for the Crown Prince and for the Chattertooth family, but we will not talk about that. There's quite a different question. What could we do with him? Endless work and drudgery lie behind my boys' performance today. No one can make his way in the world unless he works honestly and conscientiously. That is true of every profession under the

sun. You need hard work for all of them. Such work my lads have put in at football, and that is why they can score a couple of goals against the English team today. And am I to keep one of them from the game so that a young man can have a bit of fun because, begging Your Majesty's pardon, he has inherited a doorpost?"

"Do not think, Mr. Chattertooth, that the Crown Prince is a milksop. Our son has devoted himself assiduously to sport, and it is a matter of deep concern for us that he receives the best training possible."

"That is a horse of another colour, Mr. Emperor. If it is only a matter of training him, then we can take him on. We have no secrets. But I have certain conditions to make."

"What are they?"

"First, he must have the physique for football. And secondly, he must live in our family like my own lads, that is, doing the same work, getting the same food, the same discipline. From the moment he comes to us he is the youngest Chattertooth, and he won't be a prince again until he leaves us. If he agrees to all that, then I can find room for him as the first reserve for my team."

"Mr. Chattertooth, here is my hand on it. We accept, and your conditions hold good."

Father Chattertooth looked across to the grandstand to where he saw a slim but sinewy youngster. He cast an eye over the well-built figure, and with his left hand took his pipe from his mouth. The Crown Prince certainly had the body for football: all the rest could be learnt. And so old Chattertooth talked away to the Emperor of Brazil at half-time. And when the Chattertooth Eleven had won the game, the Crown Prince, their new reserve, was already waiting for them in the dressing-room.

In the evening there was a banquet at the castle where the Emperor of Brazil was residing during his stay in England, and when the Chattertooth Eleven and their reserve man were taking leave the Emperor gave Mr. Chattertooth a magnificent pipe as a souvenir. For a moment the old man was quite embarrassed, but not wishing to remain in the debt of the Emperor of Brazil he delved into his pocket and drew forth the old porcelain pipe decorated with the green tassel and the huntsman taking aim at a deer.

"Your Majesty, Mr. Emperor," he said, with the dignity peculiar to him, "I have not a meerschaum pipe, but this one, if Your Majesty does not forget to clean it often enough, will draw better than any other. The best tobacco for it is Three Kings smoking mixture; you can get it anywhere."

The Emperor accepted Chattertooth's pipe with a deep bow and presented it to the British Museum. Footballers from England, Scotland and Ireland went there to have a look at it. But old Chattertooth set about packing, and his team returned to Nether Buckwheat as champions of Europe, and with the Crown Prince of Brazil as their reserve man.

VI.   Never had the village of Nether Buckwheat been so much in the headlines as on the day on which the Chattertooth family returned with the championship of Europe in their pockets and the Crown Prince of Brazil in their team. Newspapers all over the world published maps on which the Chattertooth cottage was marked with a thick X. Special reporters sent by the papers streamed along to Nether Buckwheat in order to be able to tell millions of readers how the future Emperor of Brazil lived in the Godforsaken little Bohemian village. But however great the curiosity of the world in general, the curiosity of the people of Nether Buckwheat about their new neighbour surpassed it. They had learnt from the papers who was coming to live among them, and every day there were lively discussions in the two public houses as to what sort of a reception they should prepare.

But old Grandmother Navratil, who used to tell the children fairy-tales, was the most worried of all. For her tales were chockful of princes and princesses, and now the children besieged her with questions as to what the Prince would look like. They wanted to know if his clothes would be made of cloth of gold, and whether he would come mounted on a white horse shod with gold or in a golden coach. They would brook no denial. But what on earth could poor old Grandmother say when they asked if the Prince would have a star on his forehead and a diamond sword at this side, and whether he had already killed his dragon or was just about to sally forth into the world to perform deeds of derring-do. Grandmother of Nether Buckwheat felt as though millwheels were turning in her head. The poor old soul had never so much as caught a glimpse of a prince in the whole of her life, and now all her thrilling tales would be put to

the test by the arrival of a real live prince with royal blood in his veins. You may well imagine that she was feeling rather worried, until at last she hit upon an unexpected way out, like the shrewd old soul she was.

"Children," she said, when young and old once more had gathered around her, "you have never once asked me what land the princes and princesses in our stories come from. Well, they come, one and all, from the wonderful Never-Never-Land which lies beyond the nine mountains and the nine seas. And in Never-Never-Land it is all just as I have told you, down to the last dot on the last i. There you can meet princes walking around in golden clothes and princesses have golden stars in their hair: the queens spin flax on a golden spindle and the kings divide their lands with their sons-in-law; the animals advise and help their masters, and Simple Simon finds the crock of gold where the rainbow ends. There are dragons in the mountains breathing out fire, there are red carpets in the streets of the towns, and in the depth of the woods you can find the Springs of Youth or of Death. This land is far, far away, so far that no man has ever found his way there. No steamer can land there, no aeroplane can reach it. Only little children in their innocence go there when they fall asleep, carried over the nine seas by their guardian angels. They see all the wonderful things that I have told you about, but when they come home again they forget where they have been and what they have seen, and only remember many years later, when they are as old as I am. And then they tell the boys and girls about it, and thus it comes about that only the little children and the very old know of the happy Never-Never-Land. Other people only know the workaday world where kings and princesses have nearly died out. In this world nobody goes clad in gold, and everybody has to fend for himself; not even an ant will give him a helping hand if he is in trouble. And in this world Simple Simon has to have all his wits about him to be able to pick up a living at all. Brazil is such a country, too. I won't let you into the secret of how many mountains there are between us and Brazil, but the schoolmaster says that there is only one sea. And the people there live and die very much the same as we do, and even the Crown Prince will not look much different from the Mayor's son Jack who is studying to be a doctor in Prague."

With this speech old Grandmother Navratil rescued the fairytales, but even so the children would not believe her all at once. They still went on thinking that the Crown Prince would somehow or other be different from an ordinary student, and on Sunday they would not eat their dinner but went to the station in the little town instead to see the Chattertooths arrive. Thousands and thousands of people had gathered there: they had come from the entire countryside to stare their fill and to get to the bottom of this affair of the Crown Prince of Brazil and see what sort of a fellow this old gaffer from Nether Buckwheat was.

The railway station and the town square were crowded, and boys had climbed the rowan trees and ensconced themselves in the tops. As the train drew up in the station they could see old Chattertooth standing on the step, calmly smoking the pipe the Emperor had given him.

The fire brigade band struck up the national anthem, old Mrs. Chattertooth cried as though her heart would break, the other women all began blubbering, the local police fired off a maroon, the boys shouted out, "Welcome home the Champions," and, in short, everything was on an even more mag-

nificent scale than the Whitsuntide procession. Old Chattertooth chuckled happily to himself and waved his lambskin cap until the train came to a standstill. Then he climbed out and stood before his weeping wife.

"By all that's topsy-turvy, you are howling as though it were a funeral."

Mrs. Chattertooth only sobbed and threw her arms round her husband's neck, nearly knocking the Emperor's pipe from his mouth. At this moment their sons jumped down from the train. Each pair of them carried a trunk between them, except Honza, who was carrying a large case all by himself and got down first. Last of all, came a boy with a travelling cap on his head, and carrying his own suitcase. The Nether Buckwheat children stood staring open-mouthed, their cheers frozen on their lips.

The twelfth was the Crown Prince of Brazil, carrying a suitcase, wearing a cap, dirty from the journey... Grandmother Navratil was right. Princes clad in gold are only to be found in Never- Never-Land today.

Suddenly all the boys of the neighbourhood began to compete for the honour of carrying the luggage of the Chattertooths, and, above all, of the Prince. But old Chattertooth drove the boys off. If the Chattertooths had managed to do everything for themselves so far, they were not going to start letting people wait on them now. And so the boys had to content themselves with forming a circle round their heroes and perhaps being able to touch their clothes. Thus, in the triumphal progress home the Chattertooths carried their own luggage and the Prince did the same.

"There is good reason for it," said Father Chattertooth later in the public house. "The Emperor of Brazil has given me his son to train, and never in my born days have I seen apprentices, while they were learning their trade, waited upon. If you decide to be a tramp you have to carry your own bundle. The best king is the one who has the fewest servants."

VII.   The people of Nether Buckwheat soon grew accustomed to the presence of the exalted stranger and to the visits of the curious. In the severe, monotonous and regular life of the Chattertooth boys there was little room for pomp and show. The Crown Prince really lived with them as one of themselves. Nothing was made easier for him, although his feelings were always respected. The first day old Chattertooth looked him over carefully and tested his muscles, lungs and heart. When he saw that the Prince could run and sprint like a hare he patted him contentedly on the back

and set about training him. From Spring to Autumn the Prince was with the team, either on the field or running in the woods; in winter there was skating and tobogganning. At other times there was exercising in the barn. In the first month the Prince learnt so much of the language that he and the other boys could understand each other quite well, and it is not surprising that the whole house was full of lighthearted happiness, for the twelve boys radiated health, strength and youth, and were always up to some monkey trick or other. Once the day's training was over the ringleader was old Chat-

tertooth himself. But during the training itself there was no taking it easy: old Chattertooth kept them down to it, and at the beginning the Prince often used to ache in every limb. But his father had been right when he assured old Chattertooth that his son was no namby-pamby. He endured all the initial hardships, and after six months you could not have told him from one of the Chattertooths. His chest rounded like a bell, his head well set on his neck, his arms as hard as iron, his legs supple, lithe as a cat in all his movements, and strong as a steer, it is no wonder that the photographs of the Prince appearing in the papers of Brazil were accompanied by articles full of praise and recognition of old Chattertooth's training.

And what excitement there was when Chattertooth, sturdy old watchdog of his team, used his reserve man in a match. The Prince's appearance was reported in the newspapers of the whole world, and Father Chattertooth got more publicity for his eleven than he had ever dreamt of. Teachers, trainers and experts came streaming from every side to see how the Chattertooths were prepared for their matches. They stared and stared at the old man, but they never fathomed his secret which lay in the spirit he infused. It was a spirit of unconditional self-sacrifice making each help the other, of true brotherliness. Old Chattertooth never held forth about this, but he had consciously developed it and this above all else helped them to victory.

Their fame re-echoed round the world, and wherever they went the reserve man was there, ready to jump in in an emergency. Thus he lived inseparably with them for two years, until at last he was summoned back to Brazil to continue his studies. Almost weeping, he took cordial leave of them and went home, but he could not forget the Chattertooths and never missed a chance of a game with them. He was sent to England to study, and here he trained with the Muddlesfield team and became the most popular centre-forward in England. He lived completely under the spell of sport, and when the moment came for him to ascend the throne he was literally called there from the sportsfield. It was hard for him to leave his footballer friends and to say goodbye to the exciting life of the soccer field.

His first duty as successor to the crown was to read the speech from the throne. The Cabinet sat all night drafting the first speech of the new Emperor. Every sphere of political life had to be included in its due place, and the ministers were mopping their brows before they had written out the whole speech in fine diplomatic language. When the Prime Minister was received by the young Emperor in the morning to hand him, with expressions of deepest loyalty, the text of the speech from the throne, His Majesty interrupted him at the first sentence.

"Thank you, dear Prime Minister, but I have written the speech from the throne myself. Maybe it does not pay sufficient regard to diplomatic expressions, but it is permeated with the true spirit of our country."

And His Majesty drew a notebook from his pocket and began to read:

To My People!

As we are about to make, with all due solemnity, our political kick-off, we wish today to remind our people of the rules of the game to which we shall adhere. It is the glorious tradition of our Empire always to avoid standing offside. We wish to remain true to this honourable legacy from our forefathers, and we swear that we will never stand offside, that we will defend our colours manfully and honourably, and that we shall kick into touch, or at least for a corner, all dangers. We vow that we shall avoid any foul, and that we shall never expose our nation to the dangers of a penalty.

We shall make it our care to cultivate the three insides game, in which we shall consider the finances of our country as the best centre-forward, and trade and employment as the best insides of our Empire. We shall see that the grandstands of the population are united, one and all, in the same game, and in this we shall give preference to the close passing combination rather than the adventurous system of kick and rush. It shall be our concern that head play shall in no wise be neglected, and we hope that when the time comes for the Great Referee to blow the final whistle our Empire's score will be a very high one, and that everyone will admit that we have always played fair.

May God help us!

Hip Hip Hurrah, Hip Hip Hurrah, Hip Hip Hurrah!

VIII.   In Nether Buckwheat Grandmother Navratil had managed to keep the old fairy tales alive,
but away in the West, beyond the Herring Pond,
things were going very badly with them. Every little boy had his own little motor car as soon as he
was in trousers, the older boys were busy making
wireless sets, and, one and all, they cared for nothing but sport. They had no time for tales about
happy princes and unhappy princesses, or the other
way round, and if anyone began to say that once
upon a time there was a poor boy, they immediately broke into the tale and clamoured to know what
sports-club the poor boy had belonged to. And so
the stock of American grandmothers and grandfa-
thers who had not kept up with the times did not
stand very high with their grandchildren. Fairy
tales had become simply a drug on the market.

Until someone had a brain wave.

In the state of Oregon there lived a Czech family
that had settled there twenty-five years previously,
bringing with them a grandfather, a sly old fox who
understood children through and through. He kept
his ears open whenever they were talking together,

and the result of his eavesdropping was that he found they talked of nothing but a team called the Chattertooth Eleven. For by this time the Chattertooths were so famous that even in the western hemisphere everyone of them enjoyed the fame of a legendary hero. Then the grandfather in Oregon said to himself:

"Just wait, children, and I shall hit on the right thing for you."

When they came to him in the evening before they went to bed to ask for a story, he only smiled and launched right into the middle of things:

"You have heard of the Chattertooth Eleven, haven't you? All right. But have you heard what happened to their old Grandfather and his whistle? No, you don't know that? And yet everybody is talking about it! Well, listen. The grandfather of the Chattertooths of today, may he rest in peace, was a terribly poor boy in his childhood, and his parents had not even the little cottage where the famous Chattertooths were born. They were as poor as church mice that haven't even a candle-end to gnaw. And when their son Honza – yes, he had

the same name as his grandson, the goalkeeper –
saw that they were down to their last crust he went
to his father and said:

'Father, I want to go out into the world. By yourselves you can just manage to make ends meet, but
I am out of work, and I am only another mouth to
feed. Perhaps I shall find work somewhere in the
world, and when I come back to you I may even
have some savings to bring you.'

There was a lot of hard sense in what the boy
said and his father could not say no to him. Moth-

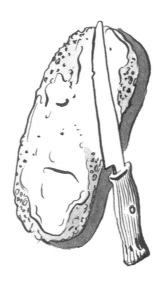

er's eyes brimmed with tears, but what mother does not cry when her son says goodbye to her? Then she gave him half a loaf and some butter that she had hastened to get, promising to pay the shopkeeper later, and Honza was ready to set out. She made the sign of the cross on his forehead and kissed him twice, and thus he went out into the world. He took to the road, cut a hazel switch, whistled when he began to feel blue, and walked on mile after mile to the rhythm of a lively march. One hill after another was left behind, and at last he found himself in a wood that seemed to go on for ever. The sun had set, and here he was still in this wretched wood, and he was beginning to feel so hungry that his stomach rumbled like a wildcat purring. When he had at last given up all hope of reaching a village, he sat down by the wayside under a tree, drew his bread from his knapsack, opened his knife and began to cut. Suddenly – lo and behold! – there stood before him an old man who said:

'You are fine and hungry, Honza, but I am still hungrier. Give me a piece of bread.'

Honza wondered where the old man had suddenly sprung from, and how on earth he knew his name, but when he saw him standing there, so poor and wretched, he handed him the loaf and knife, saying:

'Cut yourself a piece, old man. You'll find it goes down better with butter.'

The old man took the bread, cut off a piece and ate it.

'Where are you off to, Honza?' he asked then.

'I have no idea where the road will lead me. I am looking for work, but first of all I must get out of this wood.'

'It doesn't look as if you will be out of it today. It is already getting dark, and the wood is large. It would be better to sleep here.'

'And what will you do, grandpa?'

'I will sleep beside you, if you have nothing against it.'

'As if I should! But just wait a moment while I collect some dead leaves so that the ground does not feel so hard.'

Honza stood up, gathered a few armfuls of dry

leaves and prepared a bed for the old man. Then they both lay down and fell asleep. At midnight the old man awoke and his teeth were chattering.

'Brr, brr. I am so cold.' Honza opened his eyes and said:

'Take my jacket, grandpa, it will give you a little warmth.'

'Thank you, Honza. It is nice and warm. I am warmer already.'

And the old man fell asleep and it was Honza's turn to chatter his teeth with cold. But he said nothing. He only buried himself a little deeper in the dead leaves. When at last the sun rose, he began to run about to get warm again.

The old man slept long, and Honza had time to look for blackberries and wild strawberries, which he gave the old man to eat. It was certainly not a luxurious breakfast, but a hungry man can't be squeamish. Then they both rose and set off. After walking for an hour they came to crossroads.

'Honza,' said the old man, 'our ways divide here. You will go to the left and soon, you will reach a large town. I am going to the right. And because you have been so good to me and shared your bread, bed and coat with me, I will give you this whistle. Look after it well. It will bring you much luck.'

And the old man held out a small whistle to him. Honza thought to himself, 'How can this whistle bring me luck?' But he did not want to hurt the old man's feelings, and so he thrust it into his pocket and the two parted. But hardly had he gone a few steps before he felt he must look at the whistle. It seemed remarkably heavy to him. He drew it from his pocket, and then stared open-mouthed. The whistle was of pure gold! This was too great a reward for a piece of bread and butter. Honza turned, was back at the crossroads in a twinkling, and ran down the other road after the old man. But although he could hardly have gone twenty steps there was not a sign of him. Honza shouted, but an echo was the only answer. The old man had vanished as suddenly as he had appeared on the previous day.

Honza turned and continued his way, not a little puzzled by all that had happened. An hour later he was out of the wood. Before him lay an unknown land with a town in the middle. Men and carts thronged the roads. Only towards the woods, where Honza stood, there was practically no one. About halfway between the wood and the town there stood a group of people, and Honza saw that there must be a football field there. He summoned his strength and went on, and as he arrived he gathered from what he heard that the players were angry because the referee had not turned up and nobody had a whistle.

'I have a whistle,' said Honza.

'Then be our referee,' said the players.

Honza was about to explain that this was impossible when the whistle suddenly began to blow of its own accord and the players took their places.

'This is remarkably funny,' thought Honza, but before he could find any explanation the whistle blew for a second time and the game began. Honza ran onto the field and took care not to get in anybody's way. He did not need to do more, for the whistle did everything of its own accord. It whistled for out, corner, offside, goal, hands, and half-time. It blew quite fiercely if anyone indulged in rough play.

No matter how well hidden a push or a trip might be, the whistle each time sounded so persistently that the guilty man did not dare deny his fault. All the players were conscious of this and said:

'Heavens, what a referee! He sees everything. Doesn't even seem to be looking, and yet nothing escapes him. Have you ever seen the like of him before?'

And when the game was finished, they did not carry the victorious goalkeeper shoulder-high from the field, as was usual, but seized Honza and bore him in triumph to the town. The presidents of the two clubs that had been playing each other invited him to a banquet, and Honza, who had hungered and thirsted all day, got so much to eat and drink that he had to loosen his belt. But this was not the end of his luck. A week later the match for the championship was to be played in the town and there was always endless quarrelling about the referee. Each side accused anyone who was neutral of favouring the other side, and in the end they all quarrelled with each other, and the referee had reason to be thankful if the public did not set about him and beat him. And now they had found a stranger who could referee flawlessly. So they came to Honza after the banquet and begged him to remain a week longer in their town.

'Goodness!' said Honza, 'of course I could stay here, but I have nothing to eat.'

'Don't worry about that, Mr. Chattertooth,' said the business manager. 'You shall have food and quarters and, naturally, suitable honorarium.'

What they meant by honorarium Honza did not know, but he understood the matter when they paid him two gold pieces every evening for 'petty expenses.' As he already had food and lodgings provided, he spent nothing, and every evening he was able to undo a piece of the lining of his coat and sew the coins inside it. A week went by, and then Honza made such a brilliant job of it as a referee that the spectators were dumb with astonishment. They all racked their brains as to how this man, indifferent as to the outcome of the game and hardly seeming to take any notice of it, never missed a foul. But Honza knew by now that the old man he had taken under his wing was no ordinary mortal, and that there was magic in the whistle.

The whistle really brought him luck. At half-time the president of another club came to Honza and asked him to visit his town. The next day all the newspapers sang his praises, and he received one commission after another as referee. He no longer hesitated, but went here and there and took charge of the game, and since he was by no means a stupid boy he soon learnt what football was all about, and he became a referee such as the world had never seen before. He soon left off sewing the gold coins into his coat-lining, and had new clothes, and was soon quite a fine gentleman. The golden whistle served him well and faithfully, for Honza's character had not changed and he had remained the same good lad as when he left home.

But it was not always pleasant for him to exercise his office. For the whistle was inexorable and passed judgment even when it was not on the football field. And Honza was forced to recognize that in this life it is often embarassing never to let an injustice pass. It happened the first time in the office of a club. Honza was resting there during the interval, and in his presence the business manager of one club was having a discussion with the representative of another.

'Agreed!' said one of them. 'Next Sunday our teams will play against each other, and neither you nor I will put in a new player before then.'

'Done!' said the other, but then the golden whistle in Honza's pocket began to blow, for something was not in order; the other club had already put in a new player on the wing.

Both the business managers started and looked across at Honza, who had grown as red as a lobster.

'Mr. Chattertooth; please do not do such a thing to me another time,' said the business manager of the club. 'Even if you do happen to overhear something on the club premises, you should not draw attention to our tricks.'

'I am sorry,' said Honza, 'I really don't know how it happened. I will be careful another time.'

But it was of no use. If ever anything unfair was committed in his presence, the whistle began to blow, however deeply he pushed it down in his pocket. Honza was often very unhappy about it, and it often happened that unpleasantness developed because of the uncompromising whistle. One day he was strolling through a street which was so steep that two horses, harnessed to a waggon, could not draw their heavy load. The drivers stood there beating the poor beasts with the handles of their whips. Honza had not even noticed this when the whistle blew three shrill blasts to expose this rough behaviour. The drivers turned, caught sight of Honza, and set about him.

'What are you whistling for? You are trying to call the police, are you? Well, we will teach you a lesson, you wretch.'

And they rushed at Honza, who took to his heels and made off at top speed. And as he ran, the whistle blew more and more shrilly, for it was still more unfair that the two drivers should turn on one innocent person.

The longer he had it, the more the whistle brought our Honza into trouble. The more people he got to know, the more the whistle kept blowing, and above all when he walked through the teeming town the whistle hardly stopped its piercing trill. For days on end Honza would walk through the streets without coming across a just and honest man. Hardly had he exchanged a couple of sentences with someone before, as sure as eggs are eggs, the whistle would start blowing because the stranger had told a lie. Honza grew very sad on this account. When he sat alone in his room in the evening he spoke thus to himself:

'Oh Heavens, how vast is the world and how much injustice there is in it! There is not a soul on earth who wishes me well.'

He was full of bitterness as he spoke, but hardly had he said these words when from his pocket came a faint reproachful whistle. Honza jumped. He had spoken an untruth himself. Complaining thus he had done someone an injustice. So there were not only bad men. Honza fell into deep thought, and as it began to grow dark in his room the picture of Nether Buckwheat rose before his eyes. He saw his father and mother plodding on from day to day, unable to escape want, but with never a cross word passing their lips. And Honza was filled with home-sickness and longing to share the poverty of these honest souls. His comfortable life suddenly disgusted him. What good did it do him to be able to play the gentleman when his honesty brought him nothing but enemies? Home, children, home, that is a different matter altogether. 'There my golden whistle can simply become an heirloom,' thought Honza.

And Honza stood up, switched on the light, and counted his savings. He had certainly not saved a lot, but, after all, not even a judge can save a fortune, let alone a referee. Still, he had a hundred or two.

And now Honza did not waver for a moment. He paid his hotel bill and made for the railway station at once, to return to Bohemia, to home, to mother. And what a welcome he received! It is a wonder they did not smother him with their kisses. And what joy there was when he drew his banknotes from his pocket. The old people had never seen so much money in one heap in all their lives. Honza and his father put their heads together, and the next day they bought a field on the edge of the wood, and a month later they had started to build. When the cottage was ready Chattertooth married. A year later he had a son, who became father of the famous Chattertooths. Old Honza Chattertooth never left his village again. He lived an honest and upright life, and the golden whistle, which he kept for safety in the chest under his Sunday hat, never once let out a sound.

When he died, many years later, it occurred to his family that he had once possessed a golden whistle or something of the sort. They looked in the chest, but the whistle was nowhere to be found. It had gone its way with Honza Chattertooth, performing for him one last service.

Honza Chattertooth came to the Gates of Heaven and knocked. A grill was opened and a sleepy voice complained:

'Who has woken me up?'

'It's I, Honza Chattertooth, from Nether Buckwheat. I should like to come in.'

'What's the name – Honza Chattertooth?'

'Yes.'

'Wait a moment, I must look at the records.' St. Peter shut the grill again, took his big book in which the names of all sinners are written, and looked under the letter C. As he was feeling very sleepy that night, however, he looked at the wrong line, and instead of Chattertooth, Honza, Nether Buckwheat, he looked at Chattertooth, Jacob, Upper Buckwheat, And this man was a miserly wretch of a peasant, an insatiable skinflint, a morose boor, and a pickpocket. So St. Peter angrily opened the grill and bellowed out:

'You have wasted your time coming here. You have spent your whole life scraping ha'pence together. About turn and to Hell!'

He banged the grill to again. Tears came into the eyes of old Honza Chattertooth, for when had he ever hoarded money? That such an injustice should be done to him...

But before he could get his thoughts in order, at the very moment when St. Peter made his mistake, the golden whistle, which Honza had quite forgotten about, set up a piercing screech. It flew out of his pocket, fluttered about before the door of Heaven, and blew louder and more insistently. Through all the seven Heavens rang the sound of the whistle, re-echoing from star to star, and from sun to moon and down to the earth, a terrible bloodcurdling sound. It began to thunder and lighten, and the angels fluttered about like frightened doves, and above the sound of the whistle and the thunder a voice was heard saying: 'Peter, Peter, someone has been unjustly treated!' St. Peter, who was already beside himself, rubbed his eyes on his sleeves, glanced out once more, and could hardly refrain from a whispered oath.

'Good gracious me, but it is Honza!'

And he ran from the Porter's Lodge to open the door. At the same moment the whistle stopped its terrible sound, clouds and lightning disappeared, a rainbow shone over the door, and Honza Chattertooth, who had wronged nobody, entered Heaven. The baby angels began to turn somersaults because the whole business had ended so happily. And when Honza took a closer look at St. Peter, lo and behold, it was the same old man whom he had met so many years before and who had given him the magic whistle! Honza gave it back to him as he would not need it in Heaven. There were, indeed, some angels who played football, and they invited him to referee, but naturally this was a paradisaical game with no rough play, and there was never any kind of a rumpus. They floated around in circles, and one would beg the other to be so good as to give the ball a kick. And so angelically gentle were they all, the ball would have remained perpetually in one spot had it not possessed wings and fluttered of its own accord from one heavenly goal to another."

That was the fairly tale that the grandfather in Oregon thought out, and all the children admitted that it was 'jolly good'".

IX.   The Nestor of Czech poets, Vincenc Kabrna, had long been sleeping beneath the weight of his tombstone in Slavin, but the song which he had dedicated to the Chattertooth Eleven still thundered forth in triumph over all the sports fields of Europe and America, and the Chattertooths were still the heroes of the Old and New World.

A green field 'neath a blue sky,
White lines gleam.
See us here triumphant,
The Chattertooth Team!

The winds of the world had borne this song forth in all directions from the eleven Chattertooth throats. Millions of men quaked with a sense of imminent defeat when Kabrna's words, unpleasant but impressive, rang out over the turf

Long before the goalkeeper
Can stretch out his hands
The ball comes flying past him,
And in the goal it lands.

And how many teams on the Continent or on the islands scented that all was up with them when the inexorable chorus came round once more:

Stop! Shoot!
Kick the ball!
Straight into the goal 'twill fall!
Stop! Shoot!
And long before
You turn your head a goal we'll score.

There was never the slightest hope of beating the Chattertooths, but teams kept on trying, driven on by that eternal desire to achieve the impossible which is the essence of the true spirit of sport. The public, too, longed for their darlings, wanted to see them, wanted to be delighted by their play and by their skill. And so behind the scenes in the football world there was never-ending competition among the clubs for the honour and glory of playing the Nether Buckwheat lads. They vied with one another in their offers, each trying to outbid the other, and old Chattertooth grinned from ear to ear when he counted the money that flowed into his drawer from all corners of the world.

The family cottage of the Chattertooths stood there on the edge of the wood, just as it had done when old Chattertooth started training the boys, but now it was all in apple-pie order, freshly whitewashed and as lovingly cared for as a dove-cote. The surroundings had decidedly changed. In the meadow where the first ball had been kicked only a few years previously, there was now a model training ground with dressing-rooms, a gymnasium and shower-baths, and the presidents and committees of many clubs came along to study the perfection of all these arrangements. Old Chattertooth had bought up the neighbouring ground, bit by bit, and built there separate houses for each of his sons. They were jolly little dolls-houses, each with one room, a garden and a yard, and together formed a regular little family colony, the subject of much talk in the countryside and of pictures in the newspapers of the whole world. The boys themselves did not understand why their father was so keen on their having each his own small house. They felt happiest when they were together, and it never came into their heads that they could ever want to separate and each set up on his own.

"You do not yet understand," old Chattertooth would reply when they questioned him, "but one day you will find the little houses just the very thing you want."

The work of building and plastering and decorating went on, and old Chattertooth did not let it bother him that the boys were happiest when they could stretch out together in the hay or take a nap on the threshing-floor in the barn. In the meantime they had grown to manhood, and even the youngest had caught up with Honza in height and breadth of shoulder. Their father no longer kept up such a severe regime, but the lads themselves saw to it that they kept in the form they were in when they had had to fight their way into the first division of the league. Often now, especially on the day before a match, they went for a long walk instead of training.

One day they thus walked through the woods, singing and whistling as they walked. Each had some bread and butter in his pocket, and there was water to drink in the rippling woodland stream: they had all that they wanted, and they went along joyful and contented. After they had been walking a couple of hours, the green shade of the wood began to lighten and between the brown tree-trunks they saw a cornfield and a clearing. There was a sound of boys shouting and running, broken from time to time by a droning sound. The Chattertooths soon guessed what it all meant. Football!

The Chattertooth boys looked at each other and their mouths almost began to water. Half an hour's football would have been just the right thing after their walk.

They longed for the ball with every fibre of their beings. They came out of the wood. Sure enough, some peasant boys were playing there just as boys usually play. They had built a goal from their jackets, and rolled up their trouser legs and their shirtsleeves. The lines of the pitch were left to the imagination, and, as you may well imagine, this had given rise to much shouting. There was much argument, too, as to whether the ball had gone over the top of the "goalpost" or well and truly into the goal. They played with all the enthusiasm of which small boys are capable, but the main thing was that they were playing with a perfectly good leather ball well pumped up. The eyes of all the Chattertooths were fixed on this ball as they emerged from the wood. At the same moment the boys at play saw the newcomers. One of them, just about to kick the ball in, turned and caught sight of the young men emerging from the trees. The ball fell from his hands, and he stared in the direction of the wood. Full of awe, fear, and admiration, he let fall the words: "The Chattertooths!"

The others turned as one man, and it was goodbye to the game. Clustered together the youngsters stood stockstill, never taking their eyes off their heroes. Only one of them, the boy with the ball, did not lose his head. Perhaps because he was not a village boy but from the town, and quite accus-

tomed to rubbing shoulders with celebrities. When he had seen what all the fuss was about, he cried to the others:

"Get on with the game! It's not time yet!" A lot of boyish pride lay in these words. The youngster would not allow the game to be interrupted just because some grown-ups had come on the scene, whoever they might be. And still less should it be interrupted because these were the Chattertooths. True, all honour and respect was due to them, but the game was the thing, no matter who the spectators were. The Chattertooths of all people must see that others played with the same devotion as they did. As spectators there was no reason to take any particular notice of them.

"Get on with the game, can't you!"

But the town boy shouted and stormed in vain. The rest of his team seemed dumbfounded. Especially as the Chattertooths came right up to them.

"Lend us the ball for a bit, boys," said Honza to them, "and play with us."

The village boys dropped their eyes. One or two of them laughed bashfully, others dug their heels into the grass, and the boy who had been about to throw the ball in let his hands fall.

"Whose ball is it?" asked Honza.

"Mine," cried the boy from town. He said it sharply, and hastened to tuck the ball under his right arm as if to protect it.

"We should so like to play a little," said Honza. "Will you take us on?"

There was a moment of silence. The boys all looked across to their comrade from town. He stood there, upright and pale, and looked Honza Chattertooth straight in the eye. He drew a deep breath and answered in a strained voice:

"That's impossible. We can't play with you."

"Why not? Are you afraid of a beating? We will split ourselves up."

"A beating would be no disgrace. But we can't play with you."

"But won't you tell us why?"

"Because..."

"Answer. There must be a reason. What is it?"

The boy grew a little paler and then cried:

"Because you are professionals."

"What are we?"

"Yes, you are professionals, and so we can't play with you. We play for honour and you play for money. I don't want to have anything to do with you."

The Chattertooths looked at one another, and then at the boy, in indignation. No one had ever said such a thing to them before. The younger ones grew red with rage and wanted to pitch into the boy. But Honza held them back. The truth was that the Chattertooths had never thought about this question at all. The money aspect had never occurred to them. Their father had taught them football as they grew up and they played as they had been taught. And because football was a passion with them they played wherever their father took them, no matter against whom, and they had no other thought than winning the game. To beat the other team, that was the point of the game; and the Chattertooth boys exulted in winning honestly without resorting to rough play. What had money to do with it? They had never mentioned it to their father and no one had ever reproached them with it. And here stood this freckled youngster with rolled-up trouser leg, feverishly defending his ball and obviously prepared to have a tussle rather than give up his point of view.

Honza Chattertooth, captain of the invincible Chattertooth Eleven, was at a loss. There was something in the boy's tone that showed he was right, but Honza could not get to the bottom of it. All his ideas were upset by the sentence: "We play for honour and you play for money." Was it true or false? His feelings fought against it. There had never been the ghost of a desire for money among his eleven. They, too, played only for honour. And yet he thought of the thousands in his father's drawer, and he felt he could not defend himself.

There was silence for a heart-breaking moment. Honza raised his head and looked the freckled youngster in the eye.

"Sonny," he said slowly, and with unusual emphasis, "things are not as you imagine. It is true that we earned money by playing, but we do not play for money. I know that it is difficult to explain something which we cannot prove. We will not urge you to play, but think of our talk today and do not lose sight of us. Perhaps we shall meet again one day and be able to make everything clear. Best of luck to you."

Honza Chattertooth turned back towards the woods, and his ten brothers, who all felt as he did, followed him. They vanished among the trees before the eyes of the astonished boys, and for a quarter of an hour made the quickest march of their lives. Then at last Honza stopped, looked at his brothers and said:

"The Chattertooth Eleven has been beaten for the first time today, boys. And four to nil. This freckled boy was in a higher division."

The ten brothers nodded in silence, for their captain had said so, and there was no contradicting him.

X.   The adventure with the freckled youngster left its mark. The Chattertooths did not say a word more about it, but they seemed to have lost their zest in life. Gone were the times in which they chased the ball at maddest speed during their training and spent whole evenings thinking out new tricks and surprise passes. Their healthy innate high spirits had vanished, and with them their vital joy in striving and winning. They stood about morosely, went through their exercises mechanically, and played the matches that old Chattertooth had drawn up for them in his notebook as though they were a burdensome duty. Their play still reached the highest point of perfection, their technique and teamwork were breathtaking, but in all their skill and daring the spark of enthusiasm was lacking. The difference in their game was so noticeable that no number of victories could hide it from the eyes of sporting reporters.

"The Chattertooths are stale," wrote A. E. Williams, the well-known critic of *Sport*, "Do not let us be deceived by their scores, which remain magnificent. Figures are a dry formula showing only very inaccurately the relative strengths of the teams and telling us nothing whatever of the spirit of the game. And this has undergone a change with the champions. The irresistible magic with which they overcame not only their opponents but all the spectators as well, the magic of youthful freshness and joy, has vanished. Why should we be surprised at this? Anything repeated sufficiently often loses its charm and becomes a mere mechanical problem. We have observed this in the play of all professionals in the United Kingdom. Only clean, genuine amateur play, which demands all imaginable sacrifices from its followers, can give as its reward the finest thing that physical culture has to offer, the sporting spirit. Any other form of sporting activity can lead only to the deadening of this spirit. The Chattertooths are undoubtedly the finest of all the teams for whom football represents a livelihood. Thanks to the excellence of their education they have never shown any traces of the mercenary spirit which aims at goals simply for the sake of the money that each goal brings. Nevertheless they have not escaped becoming mechanical in their play because, secure from all the surprises that beset the amateur, they have worked out a perfection in which they have no rivals. The Chattertooths are stale with their own perfection. That is a tragic fate.

Let it be a serious warning to the young people of England to remember that a healthy spirit is more important in life than mere technical skill."

It is hardly probable that the Chattertooths read these lines, for they were too dispirited even to look at the papers that were sent them. Old Chattertooth himself did not need to read Williams' diagnosis to see clearly the state of his team. He had long felt that the lads no longer had their heart in their game, and he had been too surprised to be able to collect courage enough to talk to them about it. He crept around among them like a cat that is not sure of the mood of its master. The royal pipe glowed like a foundry, for he smoked like one possessed as he vainly turned the matter over in his mind. The boys said not a word, and obediently carried out his orders, but the old gaiety seemed to have left the house forever. After long turning the matter over in his mind, he decided to ask them point-blank.

They had returned home from a match one evening and had stretched themselves out in the little yard. Nero sat on Honza's lap and stared fixedly at the hencoop where the sleepy hens were pushing each other here and there as they sought the best step of the ladder to roost on. The boys lay on the ground, their arms outstretched, and stared at the clouds. They drew in deep breaths of the fragrance that the breeze wafted across the meadows from the woods. Old Chattertooth sat on the tree-stump that served as a chopping-block, twisting and turning, and at last he got it off his chest.

"It seems to me that something is wrong with the team, the deuce take it, you wretch of a captain!" he roared.

Honza played with Nero's collar.

"What do you object to, father? Haven't we won as we always do?"

"What! Winning, that's neither here nor there. I'd be no true Chattertooth if I didn't know that if things go on like this we shall soon be leaving the field with a flea in our ear. What imp of mischief has taken possession of you all? You don't talk any more, you don't sing or whistle. When you tackle the ball you do it as if you just wanted to stop it from going any further. What is the matter with you all?"

The young Chattertooths wriggled, turned from one side to another as though the ground had begun to burn them, but not one of them let out a word. But now that he had taken the bull by the horns, old Chattertooth would not be put off, and pitched into them still further.

"Even Mother has noticed that you are like different people. Not long ago she came to me and said: 'What have you been doing to the boys, Dad?' 'What on earth should I have done to them, Mařenka?' says I. 'You're all quite changed,' she said. Even Jura, her own Jura, doesn't look after her any more, she said, and began to cry, poor soul."

Matters were not really quite as old Chattertooth had described them, but he, the sly old fox, said this to shake the lads up and get them to talk. And he succeeded, for Jura, Mother's favourite, said at once:

"It's not true that I don't care for her any more. It's something quite different that's the matter. Go on, Honza, tell father what's wrong. But see to it that we get the whole thing off our chests so that we are not bothered with it any more."

Old Chattertooth's excitement could be seen only from the cloud of smoke that issued from his pipe. His voice betrayed no sign of it as he said gently and with unusual depth of feeling:

"Well, what have you on your mind, Honza lad? Make a clean breast of it."

Honza drove Nero away, half turned to his father and looked him in the eyes.

The old man started. He had not foreseen this.

"Tell me, father, how much money have you?"

"Money? Why are you bothering your head about money? I have a hundred or two, but I have never counted it properly."

"It's like this, father. You taught us to play so that we should have something to live on. Heaven knows, you did your utmost for us, and I think we have never disgraced you. But you know perfectly well that we have never played for the sake of the money. We have never known and still do not know how much you receive for a game. And we don't give it a thought. We only want to know if you and mother have enough to live on for the rest of your lives… If not, we won't waste another word on the matter and will go on playing."

Old Chattertooth smoked like a factory chimney. "And if we have enough you will not go on playing?" "Yes, in that case we shall drop football. We have always played for nothing but the honour of being first. Anything that has been made by it belongs to you. We must see to it that you and mother have enough to live on. And if you have, we should like you to tell us."

"So you play for your father and mother only? You miserable eleven, and what do you think you yourselves are going to live on?"

"You need not worry your head about us. If there's nothing else we can get jobs as trainers to clubs. They would snap us up."

"So you want to split up the most famous team in the world?"

"Yes. We don't need to have dirty-nosed little urchins with freckles telling us that they play for honour and we play for money."

"Ah, so that's where the shoe pinches. So a freckled urchin... And that is the final decision, captain?" "Yes, father." "And the team agrees?"

A grunt of agreement came from the circle of boys. The old man stood up and slowly knocked out his pipe. It was dark and the stars were beginning to come out. The old man seemed to be having some trouble with his pipe. Not a whisper was to be heard. Suddenly he turned round.

"So, that's it, is it, you young scamps? You have to play simply on my account. So that's it. Then we'll stop the business. The football can be stowed away in the loft. We'll unlace it, let out the air: it will be flat..." "Only the football will be flat, father," cried all the boys. "Everything will be flat. We'll haul down our flag... and the Chattertooth Eleven shall be 'once upon a time.'"

His chin began to quiver. The boys saw for the first time that his work was his very life. They ran to him, embracing him, begging forgiveness, trying to comfort him.

"For Heaven's sake," he suddenly said, feeling better, "at least let me fill the pipe given me by His Imperial Highness. I shan't get a second such.

There won't be any more friendly chats with crowned heads. Well, I have always expected that you would one day break up, but I thought it would be on account of a petticoat. And now, just think of it, the boys want to be amateurs. Come along to mother. She will be surprised."

That evening there was once again as much noise and confusion in the cottage as when the boys

were to go to Prague for their first match. In the hubbub the boys did not notice that the old man had slipped through the door with his wife. They stood outside in the dark, and the old man whispered instructions to her on how they were both to act.

"...and for Heaven's sake don't let them know how much we have. We shall not take it to the grave with us. What they have earned belongs to them. But they must not know that. The money might turn their heads. They are young and should only think about getting a living. Young people don't understand money. They must go out and make their own way, and when they have won the battle of life just as they have won on the field, they will understand what money is worth... And if they ever want to marry they will find their thousands very useful."

With her work-hardened hands clasped under her apron, Mrs. Chattertooth tried to swallow her tears. She listened to her husband and nodded her head in agreement. For he, the old cottager Chattertooth, was always so sure of the right thing to do that she could only wonder and clasp her hands in astonishment. So she took in what he told her, agreed to it, and then, both feeling quieter in mind, they went back to their sons in the cottage.

They were sitting there talking excitedly and making plans for the future. They had consigned to oblivion their whole reputation as footballers, and each was thinking only of what he would become, of what he would do, and how he would earn his living. Their natural faculties, driven by football into the background, were now aroused. They suddenly saw that life was much richer than they had hitherto suspected, and that they had more important duties than they had previously thought. As soon as sport ceased to be their profession and became what it truly is, a healthy game brightening and adding zest to their lives as citizens, it became clear to them that work and not sport was the centre of life. Well-trained and hardened as they were, physically and morally, they could not fail to have a sense of life's duties. They thought out all that the future could bring, and looked for ways of taking their due place in the human community as soon and completely as possible. If old Chattertooth had not sent them to bed at midnight they would have argued till morning. But even when they were in bed they were much too excited by the new vistas life opened up to them to think of sleeping. The cock had long crowed to usher in the morning as one by one they felt their eyelids getting heavier and heavier.

They slept far into the day, for old Chattertooth did not come and call them as usual. He let them sleep till midday, and greeted them with a sly smile when at last they ran shouting to the breakfast-table. Old Chattertooth let his glance wander over them as they sat at table: young, healthy, full of strength and the joy of living. Till yesterday he, too, had seen in them only footballers, material for the game, and had not thought of them in any other way. Today for the first time he realized what splendid young men they had grown to be. In his joy and pride he almost forgot that he had a surprise for them in his pocket. When they were about to rise after the meal he announced with an important expression that however betrayed nothing:

"Wait a moment, boys. Something has come for you!" He put his hand in his pocket, drew out a telegram, and laid it on the table.

XI.   A little folded piece of paper brought to a sudden end the gaiety of the boys. They looked in desperation from the mysterious telegram to the sphinx-like face of their father. Honza finally pulled himself together and opened the telegram. It was from Vincenc Maceška in London, and ran as follows:

AUSTRALIA CHALLENGES WORLD CHAMPIONSHIP MATCH STOP THREE MONTHS TIME IN SYDNEY STOP WIRE TERMS MACEŠKA

Honza handed the telegram to Josef, who quietly read the text with trembling lips and handed it to Karel. And so it was passed from hand to hand until all of them had read the unexpected offer. The world championship in Sydney in three months? The Chattertooths against Australia? The boys were almost choking with excitement. Troubled glances were thrown at their father who remained completely calm, only shifting his pipe from one corner of his mouth to the other. At last Honza broke the silence. "Well, father, and what do you say to it?"

"What is there to say?" the old man said haltingly. "It is a pity that it has come too late. But we are not going to play any more, so why should we worry ourselves about it? In any case I have been talking to mother about what we are going to do. Today I shall order a plough in the village and as soon as it is delivered I shall plough up the fine

football ground and then sow it. It should be a grand bit of ground after lying fallow for so long. But if you had not made up your minds ... by all the saints we should have to be putting our best foot forward for Australia now."

"That's certain," said all his sons as one man. "The world championship! But have we still got to fight for it?"

"Naturally. We have beaten everybody here, but we have never met the Australians, and so they have the right to challenge you. But what's the use? We'll send Maceška a telegram to say that the Chattertooths do not accept."

He spoke quietly, as though nothing had happened, but each word was secretly a stab.

"The whole business is most unpleasant because it is sure to come out, and then everybody will say that the Chattertooths were afraid to meet Australia and preferred to shut up shop altogether."

"Not that! We won't put up with that."

"What do you want to do about it, has-been team? This very week I am going to plough up the field and sow..."

"Leave us in peace, father. Surely you can't think of that at an important moment like this?"

"Why ever not? You are sick of playing, aren't you? I always had to reckon with this. As I said before, we will plough the field, harrow it, and sow..."

The eleven Chattertooths grew terribly angry. They ground their teeth with rage, and beat on the table with their fists and rolled their eyes. The cold logic of old Chattertooth made them desperate.

"Honza, captain," they called across to him, "are you going to accept that tamely? Nothing to say? Can you bear this disgrace?"

"Wait!" shouted Honza and turned to his father, "Good, father. We will plough the field, and sow. And what shall we do afterwards?"

"We must play the peasant and wait till the corn grows. We shall have plenty of time till harvest..."

"Right, father! And we must fill up this time somehow. Give me a map!"

Twenty hands were stretched over to the book-case to get out the old school atlas in which all their travels were marked in red ink. Honza opened it, and for a long time pored over a map of the world.

"I've got it: Brindisi to Bombay, thirteen days. Bombay to Sydney, twenty days. If all goes smoothly, we shall be back a month after that. That means that we can be home again before harvest."

"Well?"

"So we shall go to Australia."

"Hurra!"

A hair-raising yell sounded from ten throats. All the brothers threw themselves upon Honza in their joy. In old Chattertooth's eyes there was a look of fervent understanding, and the haste with which he kept moving his pipe from one corner of his mouth to the other was positively alarming.

"Is that your final proposal?" he finally asked. "You scallywags, the deuce of a lot of worry you have given me. You really made me fear that you were going to make a mess of your whole fine reputation."

And now the whole eleven of them threw themselves on their father who was hard put to it to keep his feet under the impact of their enthusiasm. Then they sat down again for a new council of war which went on until mother came in with the first plates of steaming soup.

The meal that followed seemed to the Chatter-tooths the finest they had ever tasted. When they had finished they all agreed that the field should be ploughed up and sown as old Chattertooth had suggested, after which the team would set out on its travels.

But the first ploughing was not as straightfor-ward as they had imagined it would be. Hardly had old Chattertooth started looking around for a plough before there was a babel of questions and gossip. In every farm, in every public house the talk turned on the same theme, and that very afternoon the rumour reached the village school. Schoolmaster Jaroušek was one of the most loyal supporters of the Chattertooths, not so much from love of football as from a fervent local patriotism. As the birthplace of the Chattertooths Nether Buckwheat had become famous throughout the world, and the schoolmaster considered it a sacred duty to feed and tend this fame by all means in his power. So at least once a week he sent little paragraphs to the *Prague News* reporting what visitors the Chattertooths had had in the last seven days, and what engagements old Chattertooth had accepted. If ever a historian wants to write a more detailed and learned account of the Chattertooths than this, he will not be able to carry out his work without first studying the correspondence corner of the *Prague News*. The schoolmaster sat at his desk and in his most delicate copperplate wrote his usual letter:

"From Nether Buckwheat. We have received the following letter from one of our regular readers. Our little hamlet of Nether Buckwheat near Kouřim has become, strange to say, the scene of events that may well be termed historic. It is public knowledge that our Bohemian folk have won resounding fame for their skill in a game called football. In this so-called football, which might more properly be called kickball, and which originated in England and demands great physical prowess of its devotees, the Chattertooth family, dubbed the Chattertooth Eleven Football Club, have won distinction. With true courage the Chattertooth Eleven has won us glory throughout the world. The whole Bohemian public has followed breathlessly its chain of successes, but for the citizens of the hamlet of Nether Buckwheat near Kouřim is reserved the unique honour of being able to say that the cradle of this famous team was rocked beneath their simple thatches. With troubled heart it is now our duty to inform the people of Bohemia that in the breasts of the Chattertooth Eleven the decision has matured to abandon football and devote themselves to rural avocations. In the next few days the gleaming steel of the ploughshare will cleave the virgin soil of the football field of the Chattertooths in Nether Buckwheat near Kouřim, the loosened soil will receive the grain, and in due course a rich harvest will be yielded up. This act, almost symbolic in its nature, means the end of the glorious career of the Chattertooth Eleven, but we, the people of Nether Buckwheat, welcome them in our midst as simple fellow-citizens. Never shall we forget that by their brave and zealous deeds and by their having once given hospitality to his Highness the Crown Prince of Brazil, the fame of Nether Buckwheat near

Kouřim has been built up, and to it we may now, with a slight alteration, apply the verse of Holy Writ: 'And thou, O Nether Buckwheat by Kouřim, art not the least among the towns of Judah.'"

The editor of the *Prague News* had not the faintest inkling of what a sensation he was unleashing with this letter. It was quoted in all the evening papers, the telegraph agencies flashed it out around the world, and the next day a wave of excitement spread through the whole of the sporting world at the news that the Chatterton Eleven would cease to exist. Then from London burst the bombshell of

the match with Australia for the world championship. In a word, the alarm sounded by the schoolmaster re-echoed round the world. How it affected the Nether Buckwheat post office is revealing. From morning to evening old Mazucha the postman was on his feet taking telegrams and express letters to the Chattertooth cottage. Distinguished sportsmen, club presidents, reporters and high public officials begged the honour of an invitation for the day when the football field would be ploughed up. Obviously this moment was regarded throughout the world as one of historic importance for European sport. Old Chattertooth was quite right when he cried out as he sorted this express correspondence:

"Bother Europe, we shall never escape it!" The next day a few gentlemen arrived from Prague, and it soon became clear that there was nothing for it but to make a great national and international festival of the ploughing up of the field. The Olympic Committee decided to form its own organizing subcommittee. Kada and Vanek, the veterans of the football field, were asked to make speeches on the occasion, and when the Minister of Education delegated Departmental Chief V. V. Štech to the committee, it was clear beyond all shadow of doubt that nothing was lacking to make the day a roaring success.

XII.   There was terrific excitement in Nether Buckwheat when the great dawn dawned. Delegations came in a never-ending stream from Kouřim: footballers, athletes of all sorts, sprinters and runners, weight-putters and javelin throwers, jumpers and wrestlers, rowers, cyclists, boxers, marksmen, swimmers, motor-cyclists, gliders and pilots, mountaineers, billiard players, chess champions, motorists, jockeys, yachtsmen, fencers, tennis champions, basketball players, skaters, ice-hockey players, polo and rugby players, golfers, cricketers, canary, pigeon and dog fanciers, anglers and ju-jitsu wrestlers. They came rolling along the roads and lanes, driving all sorts of contraptions, and the woods around Nether Buckwheat re-echoed with a dozen different languages. The Chattertooth sports

field was decorated with flags, and a platform for speakers had been erected over by the northern goalposts. On every side there were wandering hawkers selling sausages, sweets and lemonade. At ten o'clock the emerald field was black with a countless host of visitors. At a quarter to eleven the president of the festival committee led a white-haired old man onto the platform.

"Kada! That is Kada!" roared the crowd, and old Kada went on bowing and bowing.

Some time passed before the cheering died down and the trembling old man could read his speech. In the midst of an equally violent storm of applause his place was taken by Vanik, who, bent with age, could not hold back his tears. But the applause seemed as though it would never stop when the Chattertooth Eleven, with their gently blushing father in their midst, appeared on the platform. Honza, the captain, thanked those present in a few words and was turning to leave when a fresh storm of cheers broke out. Eleven young girls in light sports dresses climbed the platform. They were the invincible world record holders in running, from a hundred yards to half a mile, in high and long jumping, in putting the weight and javelin-throwing. They had come to thank the champion footballers, in the name of all sportswomen, for their example and their achievement, and each pinned on the Chattertooths a little festal badge designed by the sculptor Gutfreund. The Chattertooths were much surprised at this unexpected decoration and their hearts beat loudly in their breasts as the pretty champions pinned the badges on. At the same moment V. V. Štech made a sign and the military band burst forth with the strains of the Chattertooth Anthem.

At last the heroes of the day could leave the platform to perform the real ceremony. In the north-east corner of the field stood a garlanded plough to which were harnessed two horses from the royal stud of Trakehnen, famous stallions in their days, but now grown gentle with age.

Old Chattertooth took the bridle from the groom. He had reserved for himself the honour of guiding the plough. The honour of drawing the first furrow was reserved for the representative of the Government, the Minister of National Health, and everyone had to admit that he was an astonishingly good hand with a plough. The return furrow was ploughed by the British Minister, and then it was the turn of the President of the Olympic Committee, the Deputy President of the International Football Federation, and the President of the Central Committee of Sports Clubs. Last came the turn of the humble but never-to-be-forgotten schoolmaster, Mr. Jaroušek, the first teacher of the heroic Chattertooth Eleven.

The whole model playing field was now scored with furrows, the upturned earth gleamed in the spring sunshine, and the crows from the nearby woods took their toll of worms.

In the meantime the band had settled down on the edge of the wood, and the people followed their example in the meadows and pastures, and a vast picnic ended the first and official part of the ceremonies. In the afternoon there was dancing, and in the evening the delegations left for the railway station after the Chattertooth Anthem had once more been sung.

The blue velvet of evening enfolded the whole countryside, now quiet once more. Through the early twilight gleamed the white walls of the Chattertooth cottage, which, flanked by the Nether Buckwheat woods, appeared lonelier than ever.

This made it seem the cosier and snugger inside the old cottage, where unwonted lights were gleaming in all the windows. At the long table in the best parlour sat eleven Chattertooths and eleven girls, everyone of them a worldchampion. Old Chattertooth had not allowed the girls who had given them such a pleasant surprise to go to the station amid the terrible crush of people. In league with the representatives of their clubs he had persuaded them to be his guests. In the afternoon two little white houses had been prepared to receive them, and in the evening, when everyone else had gone home, the girl sports champions sat down to the family supper with the football champions.

Some kind of peculiar magic seemed to have enveloped the young people. Up to this time Chattertooth's boys had never really got to know any girls. If one did by chance turn up, her affectation made her seem silly to them. They seemed only intent on pleasing, and danced around the boys in order to catch one of them, for most girls were crazy about the Chattertooths. The healthy, sensible and proud boys hated all this, and moreover, were afraid that one or other of them might get caught and be lost to the team. This made them enjoy all the more the company of girls who did not flirt or talk rubbish. They knew from practice how to run and how to breathe, they asked the Chattertooth boys about their experiences and exercises, and the boys told their new friends how to acquire elasticity and when it was best to have massage. Everybody at the table was brought into the best of spirits by this exchange of expert knowledge and the calling up of happy memories of travels and sport. When the Chattertooths had seen the girls to their little houses and said goodnight to them, it was clear to them that they had never before enjoyed such a jolly and friendly talk. And old Chattertooth eagerly upheld them in this view, and when the boys had stretched themselves out on their camp beds he walked up and down before the threshold drawing at his royal pipe. It was past midnight when the door creaked and Mother Chattertooth called gently to him to go along to bed.

"In a minute, Mother. I only want to see if all is quiet over there where the girls are. Come a couple of steps with me. It is quite warm."

Mrs. Chattertooth slipped out, Nero came from his kennel, and all three walked along the edge of the fallow field to the little houses at the other side. Divine peace and quiet reigned there, all the lights were out and nothing was stirring. The Chattertooth couple made their way back. Halfway to the cottage, old Chattertooth paused:

"Girls and boys, they are all sleeping free of care. May God grant that they are happily launched in life on the crest of their wave of youthful fame."

"God grant it, father," whispered Mrs. Chattertooth. Then both crept on tiptoe into the sleeping house.

XIII.   Hail to the Sea! And to the firmament, the sun, and to the unending vistas. Not a wave to be seen in these days of glowing sunshine and oppressive heat. The sea is dead, as if killed by the vertical shafts of light that pierce it: in vain the bow of the ship cleaves it on its endless journey. Foam springs up on either side of the ship, and behind it two long furrows mark its wake as far as the eye can see. Apart from that everything is dead, bound in motionless sleep. The movement of the ship is almost imperceptible. Only from time to time rosy outlines of mountains appear on the horizon, but maybe they are a dream, imagination, a play of light. From time to time the ship approaches them and glides along the coast. Then a red-gold desert comes into sight, with here and there a few palm trees and a collection of huts, men in white burnouses, women in bright cotton robes, and long strings of camels, swaying one behind another as they amble along, tied together.

The Chattertooths have stretched themselves out in the deck-chairs in the shadow of an awning, and with eyes half shut against the painful glare they stare silently at the passing panorama of the Arabian coast. When the sultriness and raging thirst become unbearable they think sadly of the rich beauty of the Mediterranean Sea. Hardly a week ago they had been thinking that the heat there was too great, but how mild that region had been compared with the hell of the Red Sea. The sea had been stained with a hundred hues. Tender clouds had scudded across the sky. Waves had broken into a cloud of foam, as they chased each other, had sunk and vanished and reared their heads afresh. The Chattertooths droop their eyelids and their memories wander still further back, back to the fragrant pine forests and the woods of sappy oaks, back to the meadows where the buttercups gleam and the brook meanders from alder to alder, back to the ploughed-up sportsfield at the edge of the wood, back to the cottage and mother with her half-humorous grumbling. Never have they left her, poor soul, for such a long time. Only Nero, with his coaxing ways, stays at home with her, and he, too, is getting old and loves to stretch out lazily doing nothing. He can only manage a hoarse bark when a stranger passes by. There is one ray of comfort: at the station the eleven jolly girls promised to take it in turns to go to Nether

Buckwheat to amuse and comfort poor lonely Mother Chattertooth. If it weren't for that, mother would have to sit all alone on the threshold as the mist began to rise from the meadows and the pine-woods, and with folded hands look up to the gleaming stars shining above the wonderful land to which her husband and sons had gone forth for the last time for the sake of honour and glory.

The evenings on board the *Princess Mary* are different. The cool air draws the people out of the hiding places to which they have retired to escape the heat and sultriness. Lanterns gleam and the ship's band strikes up and the passengers enjoy a few hours of social life. As the passengers are mostly English men and women, the Chattertooths are soon surrounded by a circle of admirers. Even the thin English teacher, who has been transferred to a school in Benares, feels her heart beat faster when she hears that these eleven youngsters are world record breakers. The whole evening long the boys are surrounded by new acquaintances and admirers, and old Chattertooth and one of the other passengers get as thick as thieves.

It had started on the evening of the day on which they left Brindisi. The boys, drunk with the novelty offered them by the engines of a large ocean-going liner, explored every corner of this ship and stuck their noses everywhere, while old Chattertooth dragged his deck-chair as far forward as possible and settled down comfortably. Hardly a minute had passed before a broad-shouldered giant sat down beside him. His trousers needed pressing, he had vast boots, and in his mouth was a pipe that was an exact replica of Chattertooth's royal one. He began speaking English in a voice that rasped like a wheelbarrow that needs oiling.

"Are you Mr. Chattertooth?"

Old Chattertooth reviewed his whole array of English words, made his choice quickly and decisively, and said with an affirmative nod:

"Yes."

"I am Colonel Ward of the Anglo-Indian army," the giant thereupon said. "I like the look of you, and so I feel like sitting with you here. What do you think about it, Mr. Chattertooth?"

This speech seemed to the old man to be bris-ding with difficulties, and his whole English vocabulary was thrown into disorder. Finally the saving word came into his mind, and he said:

"Yes."

Thereupon he exchanged a terribly long handshake with Colonel Ward. The Colonel stretched himself out in a deck-chair beside Chattertooth. The old man from Nether Buckwheat was already in a panic as to what would happen once Colonel Ward started talking, but that just did not happen. The Colonel sat there and smoked: old Chattertooth sat there and smoked. They both smoked, a company of two. An hour had passed. The Colonel raised his hand and pointed to a white bird flying in circles round the bows and said:

"Seagull."

Chattertooth nodded in agreement.

"Yes."

An hour later Chattertooth caught sight of a porpoise bobbing up and down in the water. He looked at it for a while, and then he raised his hand and said quietly:

"The fish."

Colonel Ward nodded sententiously.

"Yes."

And again they sat there, smoking. When they first approached the coast of the Red Sea, Colonel Ward said:

"Arabia."

And Chattertooth answered:

"Yes."

Then Chattertooth pointed with his pipe towards the shore and said:

"The camel."

The Colonel assented:

"Yes."

One morning they passed the Straits of Aden and were in the Indian Ocean. At last there was once more a real sea, with foaming waves eternally roaring and rearing. As if filled with fresh desire, the *Princess Mary* bounded forward. When the Gulf of Aden had been left behind there was nothing to be seen but waves, often rising to vast heights, and with a slow pitch and toss the ship ploughed its way through the watery hills and valleys. Old Chattertooth and Colonel Ward never abandoned their headquarters. They remained on their swaying perch which was nosing its way steadily south-westwards. They left their seats only to eat and sleep, and during the lovely nights they often sat there till long after midnight.

Until at last the enchantment of the night was pierced by an array of lights, small and large, that rose before their eyes; a beam of light, striped green and white, swept the sea, the ship's syren began to wail, and Colonel Ward said:

"Colombo."

And old Chattertooth added:

"The end."

And both nodded and said:

"Yes."

In the morning they took leave of each other with endless handshaking, but never a word passed between them. Both felt that here was eternal friendship, and that till their death neither would find another with whom he could so freely exchange ideas as he had done on this journey from Italy to Ceylon. They wished each other Godspeed, and they knew they would never meet again, for Ward was going somewhere in the depths of India, and the *Princess Mary* left Colombo the same evening to continue her journey to Sydney.

XIV.   Announcements in the newspapers, posters, leaflets, newsreels, slides throwing illuminated publicity puffs on to the walls of the houses at night, neon lights, millions of photographs, leading articles in the papers, all these helped to prepare Australia two months in advance for the great match with the Chattertooths. The progress of their journey, reported by radio despatch day by day, was followed with interest, and at the bookmakers vast bets for and against began to pile up. The betting was five to one on Australia when the best sports reporter, a certain G. B. Greenwood, succeeded in smuggling himself onto the *Princess Mary* and spying on the Chattertooths as they played on deck or rubbed themselves under the showers. The result of his observations was a despatch that brought the odds on Australia down to three to one. And when the Chattertooths themselves appeared on the landing stage before the eyes of the vast crowd that had gathered to welcome them in Sydney, the odds on Australia dropped to not more than one and a half to one. But then the patriotic sportsmen intervened and so inflamed their countrymen in a fiery publicity campaign that the final betting was six to one on Australia.

A week before the match the town was already full of visitors who had come to see the great game. More steamers arrived daily in the harbour, disgorging trippers who in the end had to spend the night in attics, in boats, or in tents outside the town. On the eve of the match the public forced the entry of the Stadium, swept in like a frightful wave and took possession of the unreserved seats to make sure of getting a place. Ten thousand people slept there, huddled on the stone seats, and early next day an army of hawkers set up their stalls. In the morning two bands were sent into the Stadium to keep the excited crowd in a good temper with brisk marches and foxtrots. All the same there were quarrels and disputes, and a good many fists were injured in fighting for better places.

From midday onwards the public in the grandstands formed themselves into speaking choirs. Short sentences and cries such as:

"Lick the Chattertooths," or "Kangaroos against Europe," were roared out rhythmically by the whole grandstand. A fine competition arose between the north and the south grandstands as to which could shout the louder. There were such orgies of shouting from thousands of throats bellowing like one that the bands stopped playing and contented themselves with a fanfare after a specially deafening roar from the crowd. By two o'clock nobody could produce more than a hoarse whisper, and the shouting match between the north and the south remained undecided.

By this time the Stadium was so full that it was like the seething crater of a volcano. At half-past two the police shut the gates. Thousands of stragglers who found the gates shut against them began to rage and storm outside. But the gates were shut immovably upon them, and they were doomed to walk up and down outside the forbidden paradise, guessing what was happening inside from chance shouts, thunders of applause, whistles, and catcalls.

The noise and shouting were exceptionally confused: they came in a roar, like surf breaking over the high wall of the Stadium. There was an hour and a quarter before the start of the game, and those who had come too late settled down on the grass after fruitless attempts to smuggle themselves in. At two minutes past four their talk was interrupted by a roar of applause that sounded like a tropical thunder-shower. It was a round of greeting sweeping the arena – obviously the Chattertooths had arrived. Three minutes, and another salvo of applause, a sound of tramping, and many voices raised in a shout – the champions of Australia were entering the field. And then suddenly – an endless, tantalizing, deathlike silence. Those exiled outside the walls grew pale with excitement, and with heads outstretched tried to catch the smallest sound from within. But it was as quiet as if a vast glass dome had been let down invisibly over the whole hundred and sixty thousand spectators.

The exiled ones kept looking at their watches: but the hands crept on like snails.

Suddenly they all started. A sharp whistle cut the air. The thud of a ball being kicked was heard. The exiled ones kept staring fixedly in the direction from which the sounds came.

For a moment a light brown ball was seen soaring like a rocket high above the outside wall. It glistened brightly in the sunshine and sank silently back. Two sharp whistles followed.

At this moment three boys ran across the bend of the main road that led to the suburbs. One behind another, they ran with the long stride of the athlete, raising their legs well and dropping resiliency down onto their toes. A ragged boy with dark curls and a scarlet cap led and the others followed at even distances. Half-way to the Stadium the last boy overtook the second, and together they caught up the leader and covered the last part of the way in a line. They stopped at the first group of people outside the gates.

"Herald! Extra!"

"Teams enter the field!"

"First minutes of the match! *Herald! Herald!*"

The piercing cries from the three young throats gave the excited listeners a shock. Was it possible that already...? They threw themselves onto the papers. Yes, here it was in black and white. A record of journalistic slickness. Paragraph by paragraph, with sub-headings in heavy print.

"The phenomenal Chattertooth Eleven in their

white shirts with their national tricolour on the left breast are running like a snake on to the green turf. The classical figures of the eleven athletes…"

"Again thunderous applause breaks out. Old Short, incomparable Hiram Girford Short, leads the row of divinely lithe Australians in their red shirts…"

"John Herbert Nearing is pushing back his cap and lighting his pipe. Let us cast a rapid glance over the wonderful field where the twenty-two rivals stand like statues. A sharp whistle startles us. The teams are in motion."

"The first minutes are in our favour!"

The *Herald* was snatched from hand to hand, and men clustered round every copy like wasps round overripe apricots. The three ragged boys ran here and there and had not hands enough to stick the coins in their pockets. After a couple of minutes they had not a paper left. The giant gate rose before them – shut. They looked at each other and their faces grew longer and longer.

"Here's a fine mess, Sammy!" said the boy who had been third in the row to the dark-haired boy.

"And you swore to us that we should be able to slip inside with the papers as easy as anything."

With dark looks Sammy went up to the gate. It was no use. It was properly locked. Sammy looked desperately at his two comrades who were waiting for him to say the word. Behind the wall, in the far distance, a whistle sounded. That could mean an out, a corner, or a foul. It didn't bear thinking about. Sammy Spargo not see a match!

"You two go left round the Stadium and I will run round to the right, and we'll look for a hole somewhere. We'll meet at the other side."

The boys obediently ran off, and Sammy trotted to the right. The eagle eye of the newspaper boy swept the walls for a hole through which it would be possible to slip in. Nothing met his eye but smooth grey concrete broken here and there by a closed gate. And the ball inside could be heard swishing through the air.

He was more than half-way round when he met the grubby Jennings and lanky Buthurst.

"Have you found anything?"

"Nothing. And you?"

"Nothing."

All three cried this out in the same breath. Little Jennings was nearly crying. Sammy Spargo stamped in fury. There was no gate on the side of the Stadium where they were. The fields began here, and there was no road. There were no people here either. There was only a ditch from which others ran out along the edges of the fields. Sammy Spargo looked round helplessly. Suddenly his eyes shone.

"Do you mean to say that's no good?"

His two friends looked where he was pointing. True, how on earth could they have overlooked it? Fifty paces from them the ground rose. Not high enough for them to be able to see over the wall from it, but at its highest point stood a lonely tree!

With cries of joy they jumped across the ditch and raced up the ridge to the higher ground. But alas! The trunk of the vast eucalyptus was so thick that the boys could not climb it. And it was getting near the end of the first half! This was no time for hesitation.

"Forward, Buthurst. Stand by the tree and press hard against the trunk! Jennings, climb up his back and stand firmly on his shoulders. Press yourself hard against the trunk, too. Now I shall climb up over you both, and then somehow or other I shall be able to reach a branch. Don't wobble, Buthurst, the weight is nothing for a lump like you. Look here, Jennings, when I am up, you've got to hold on to my feet and then Buthurst climbs up on to you. Stick it, fellows. Now. Ready? Here goes!"

Sammy Spargo had managed to catch hold of a small branch with his left hand, and with a bold movement to swing up to it, so that he now lay with half his body across the main branch. His legs hung down, and Jennings was feeling for them. But Sammy Spargo was not conscious of this. He was staring with all his might over the heads of the spectators to where three-quarters of the field lay before his eyes. Jennings had at last managed to catch hold of him, and Buthurst, after spitting on his hands, had sprung onto Jennings as he reared himself up.

At that moment a thunderous roar broke out. Sammy Spargo shouted, his hands lost their grip, and he slipped down the trunk of the tree. Buthurst and Jennings rolled onto the grass. Sammy fell on top of them. The thunderous roar had changed to a never-ceasing yell. Three battered boys rose to their feet. The two boys threw themselves onto Sammy.

"What is it? What did you see? What's happened?"

Sammy Spargo stood there pale with excitement, his eyes glazed as if he were under the spell of a vision he had seen in the Stadium.

"Sammy, for heaven's sake, tell us! What's happened?"

At last he turned to them and shouted:

"Australia has just got a goal!"

XV.   Three seconds before one hundred and sixty thousand Australians let out their full-throated yell of victory, there had been a light snapping sound in the seats of honour: Father Chattertooth had bitten through the stem of the royal pipe. In this fraction of a second that seasoned old footballer had grasped that things were going badly. More by instinct than by any process of reasoning he had seen that a goal would be scored and that it was impossible to stop it. The blame was due to Tonik's slowness and to the misjudgment of Jura who was playing left back. As it seemed at first that the attack would come from the middle, the right back was too far forward when the Australian right centred the ball. And so when the ball flew towards the goal in a lovely curve and went to old Short un-marked in the middle, a goal was already assured. Just for a fraction of a second one thought Short might shoot past the post or at the goalkeeper. Honza indeed twice sprang forward to lessen the Australian's shooting space, but Short was already at the ball like a madman. It rolled up to him so perfectly that it fell on to his right instep just as he swung his foot forward, and then the ball flew into the net. It went past Honza's right limb, the keen-est shot that old Chattertooth had ever seen. The world went dark before his eyes, his knees grew weak, and his heart missed a beat. He could not even bring out a curse. Mechanically he puffed at his pipe, but it no longer drew, for he had bitten it in two.

The shouts of the spectators lasted at least twelve minutes. The game had long been resumed, but the people in the grandstands were stamping, dan-cing, and hugging each other. Old Chattertooth, a little pale, looked motionless down into the field. No, he was not mistaken. The boys were playing quite differently today. Maybe they were feeling

G

GOAAAL GOOOOAL

GOAAAL GÓÓAL

GOOAAL

slack after the journey, or their hearts weren't in it: at any rate, something was wrong. It was still a grand game, and the spectators were wild with enthusiasm, but the real fire was lacking, that playing as if possessed. The Reds, on the other hand, were playing like eleven demons, and the whole of the first half the Chattertooths were on the defensive.

When the referee blew his whistle for half-time with the Australians leading one to nil, the Chattertooths went back to their dressing-room completely overcome. Not one of them spoke a word. They threw themselves on to the benches, and Honza kept on blowing his nose to keep back the tears that sprang to his eyes. In the neighbouring room a swarm of masseurs and trainers had seized on the exhausted Australians and were refreshing them with massage and cheery words. In the Chattertooth dressing-room there was dead silence, and the shadow of impending defeat lay across the Nether Buckwheat Eleven. Where on earth was their father? He of all people, who was always waiting for them in the dressing-room, was missing today. The minutes passed, but no sign of their father.

"O Heavens! Suppose something has happened to him!" Frantik said with fear in his voice.

They were all frightened. His absence could not indeed be explained in any other way. Panic seized them. They sprang from their seats and ran to the door. A shrill, long-drawn whistle was sounding.

The referee was blowing for them to appear for the second half. But the Chattertooths had only one thought in their heads. What had happened to their father?

At this moment old Chattertooth entered.

"Father, father dear!"

Overcome with love and devotion they ran towards him. He stood before them, a little red, and could hardly escape being smothered with their embraces.

"Now, now, you young fools, wait a moment, can't you."

They felt that he wanted to say something to them. And involuntarily they dropped their eyes. But their father was not angry. His voice sounded loving, unusually loving perhaps.

"Wait a moment, boys, don't kill me! Well, I was taking a look at you when you were playing just now. Very good, very good, really. I have never seen such a performance from you before..."

Tonik looked suspiciously at him. This honey-sweet tone told him nothing. But father continued:

"Really an admirable game! Nice speed, passing

and shooting. You have certainly given me a great deal of pleasure. A fat old gentleman came up to me and told me that here in Sydney they have a club for Fifteen Stoners. He said they often play football, and couldn't he fix up a match with us in the coming week. Not earlier, so that you could have time to rest a bit and put up some sort of a show against them. An elderly lady came to me as well. She belongs to a basket-ball club. She told me to ask you if that wouldn't suit you better, rather than mixing yourselves up with footballers. And then I heard two grandmothers arguing as to whether in their young days the players used to miss the ball as often as the Europeans do today..."

"Father!"

It was more a strangled sob than a cry. They were all nearly bursting with rage. Father Chatter-tooth dropped his biting tone. He suddenly felt soft-hearted.

"I have bitten through the pipe of His Highness the Emperor of Brazil on your account, you young wretches. You'll catch it when I tell your mother..."

They could bear it no longer, but ran out on to the field where the referee was blowing his whistle furiously and all the spectators were shouting for the wiping up of the Chattertooths. Tonik stopped before the exit.

"Boys, for Heaven's sake..."

This was the last chance. All the boys felt the importance of the occasion. They dried their eyes with their sleeves and shook hands with each other in silence.

Then they went in and played.

Played like a thunderstorm let loose. There were moments when the Australians stopped short in the middle of a rush in order to see what was really happening. Eight men charged across the field like a whirlwind, with an invisible ball that finally landed in the goal. The defence? A white wall of eleven men. Passing? It could no longer be seen. At a mad pace play shifted from goal to goal. The spectators held their breath. It was no longer a question of eleven men who played with a ball: the ball itself seemed to have taken on life, bewitched and filled with a demoniac desire to beat the newest continent. In incalculable bounds it raced backwards and forwards, right and left, up and down, avoided the Australians, rolled towards the Whites, leapt aside if ever a red shirt sprang forward, made its way up the field, sometimes at an amble, sometimes like lightning, a small spherical devil in the service of the Whites.

The first goal came in the first three minutes. It was not even shot, for Karel, racing forward quicker than the ball itself, bore it into the net against his chest. The second goal, which gave the Chatter-

tooths the lead, was shot by Josef from the wing. The ball hit the upright and then landed in the opposite corner of the net. The third goal, kicked from thirty-five yards, went to Tonik, who shot when nobody was dreaming of a goal. The fourth goal was headed in by Frantik from a corner. The fifth goal, the finest of all, is recorded in the photographic archives of the Federation. It was a pile-driver by Jura. The goalkeeper hurled himself at the ball. He caught it, but it was travelling at such a speed that his weight and strength were as nothing to it, and the giant was bowled round clean into the net. When the unhappy wretch hit the ground, his body with the ball still in his arms was well over the line. The sixth goal was scored by the defeated Australians themselves. Four more goals were disallowed by the referee on the grounds of offside. But there were still eight minutes to go, and that was sufficient for Josef and Jaroslav to shoot the seventh, eighth and ninth goals.

"Where are your fifteen stoners?" cried the radiant boys to their father as they marched past the seats of honour on their way to their dressing-room.

"They have all burst, every one of them, you infernal world of champions!"

Thus in a blaze of glory ended the championship match which the boys imagined would be their last.

But in that they were mistaken.

XVI.   The *Argo,* a mail steamer of the Pacific Ocean Line plying between San Francisco, Auckland and South-East Australia, had been in heavy seas for a couple of days. She had left Honolulu in the Sandwich Islands in the best of weather, and should, according to schedule, reach Pago-Pago on Tituila in the Samoan Archipelago seven days later. On the fourth day she crossed the Line, but the usual ceremonies by crew and passengers did not take place for the storm which had raged since the morning had driven all the passengers to their cabins. Only the most seasoned among them, tied to something firm on deck, dared face the violent gale and watch the raging billows as they broke over the rolling steamer in wild rage, tossing the ship from peak to trough. In living memory there had not been such a storm in these latitudes, for the fury of the Monsoons normally ended at the latitude of the Fiji Islands. The *Argo* ploughed her way through the heavy seas, creaking and groaning, and the westerly gale drove her off the south-west course she was to follow.

"We have been driven pretty far eastwards," said Captain Grindstone at lunch to the few passengers who, wet through, had held out so long. "The *Argo* is a tough ship, but with such a storm raging it is better to let her go with the wind."

"Well, there is room enough here to go a bit off your course," Mr. Scrooge roared into his ear in reply. Mr. Scrooge was making the voyage for the twenty-second time. "But I shouldn't like to be between the New Caledonians and the Solomon Islands. We should have been a wreck there long ago."

Captain Grindstone nodded, touched the peak of his cap with one finger in farewell, and tried to reach between decks in a lull between the blasts of wind. But he did not get so far. As he passed the radio cabin, the door was opened and the wireless operator called the captain in. He was there exactly eight minutes, and when he came out he did not proceed on his way, but went at top speed to the bridge.

"Anything happened?" asked Mr. Scrooge as he raced past the few people who remained obstinately on deck.

"I have received a message," cried the Captain. "Come down into the saloon and I will tell you about it."

They went down. The air in the saloon was so thick that you could cut it with a knife, but here at least you could talk in a normal voice, and the passengers sat down expectantly. Grindstone soon appeared and was at once besieged with questions. He did not answer at once, but drew a paper from his pocket.

"I am sorry, gentlemen, but we shall be even later than we thought. We have just picked up distress signals by wireless from the SS *Timor,* which is in trouble. She has run aground somewhere off Manahako Island and has sent out an S O S."

"You will of course answer the call, Captain?" inquired the worthy Mr. G. L. Fisher, who was just returning from the Congress of the Friends of Universal Brotherhood in Canada.

"I have already given orders. I don't think there is any other ship that can reach the *Timor.*"

"When do you think we shall reach her?" asked Mr. Scrooge. "Hardly before midday tomorrow."

"Merciful Heavens! Can the *Timor* hold out so long?" cried the worthy Mr. Fisher.

"It's hard to say. But I have already informed her that we are on our way."

"Do you know the ship, Captain?"

"I couldn't give her tonnage offhand, but I have seen her time and again in Brisbane. Scott and Sturdy launched her twenty years ago in Liverpool. She makes a steady nine knots, but that is no good on the main routes these days. So she's been put on the line Brisbane–New Caledonia–Fiji Islands–Honolulu-Vancouver. She does an honest job of work, and old Elias Sweet has always managed to pull her through the tradewinds."

"You just said that her route is west of ours, but Manahaki lies east."

"That shows you how it was blowing yesterday on this side of the Line. Sweet wirelessed that she was caught off the Tokelau Islands and then drifted east. They got past the Society Islands all right, but then the *Timor* struck a reef north of Rakahanga."

"Hm, *Timor, Timor*" growled Mr. Scrooge. "I seem to have heard this name somewhere or other recently. *Timor* – Why, isn't that the ship the Chattertooths left Australia on?"

"Quite right," nodded the Captain. "As Sweet's message said, they are the only passengers on board."

All present leapt up at his words.

"Captain, you won't let the Chattertooths drown? What did you say. Midday? No, you must get there earlier. In the morning! At dawn! Heavens! Nine to one, and now they're to be drowned! The *Argo* can make it, can't she? If it means using more coal, we'll all pay."

Captain Grindstone could hardly ward off the flood of questions. But new questions stopped short on everybody's lips for the door opened and the wireless operator saluted and handed the Captain a new message. Grindstone glanced at it and then read aloud:

"God bless you for your decision. You are our only hope, but you will have to make haste. The *Timor* is stranded on a reef and cannot get away in the face of the terrible surf. We have closed the lower bulkheads, but the ship may break in two during the night. The brave Chattertooths are working with the crew, but salvation is impossible unless help arrives in time. All our signals have remained unanswered. The *Argo* is the only steamer

we have contacted. May divine Providence give you wings."

There was silence for a while. Then Mr. Scrooge said:

"What is our speed, Captain?"

"A bare eight knots with this sea."

"A hundred pounds to the fund for Sailors' Widows if it is increased to ten!"

"Stop the storm, Mr. Scrooge, and the *Argo* will make twelve."

"Storm or no storm, we must be off Rakahanga by nightfall!"

"We will do our utmost. But we cannot get there before eleven o'clock tomorrow morning."

The Captain left them, and the passengers walked excitedly up and down in the saloon. The news soon penetrated to the cabins, and many deathly pale passengers crept into the saloon to share the talk.

At four o'clock the Captain demanded a cheque for one hundred pounds from Mr. Scrooge. The *Argo* had reached a speed of ten knots. At five o'clock a new wireless message was picked up.

"Storm is not abating, the leak is increasing. Impossible to get the lifeboats clear. Deck destroyed and everything washed away. We pray God to give you good speed. We are in His hands. Hurry."

At eight o'clock the wind sank a little. The *Argo* increased her speed to eleven and a half knots. Then came a fresh despatch.

"Tried to lower the boats. All of them smashed against the side of the *Timor*. Have lost fourteen of the crew. Wave after wave is breaking over the deck and the ship is three parts full of water. Sinking slowly but surely."

The *Argo* answered:

"Hold on at any price. We are speeding to you and will be there tomorrow morning."

The *Timor* answered:

"Tomorrow morning is too late, God be with us."

Then followed silence.

The funnels of the *Argo* belched forth millions of sparks into the night. The deck was covered with groups of passengers. From time to time someone would go up to the captain.

"How many knots, Captain?"

"Twelve and a half."

"Can't you increase it?"

"The boilers would burst."

And again silence descended on the ship and people stared without a word into the hopeless darkness.

An hour before midnight another message was picked up.

"The *Timor* is nearly under water. We are building rafts on which we are not likely to be able to escape. But still we work on. The crew is not in despair for our passengers are setting an excellent example. The bond of imminent death has linked the crew and the twelve Chattertooths. God reward them for all they have done for us in our last hour."

The *Argo* answered:

"Heroes of the *Timor*, hold on. The wind here has sunk and will soon abate where you are. Tell the world champions that the passengers and the crew of the *Argo* are full of admiration for them. We are doing everything to get to you in time. Travelling at thirteen and a half knots. Hold out till midnight, and courage, courage, courage!"

At five minutes to midnight there was a fresh message.

"The *Timor* has broken in two. I, Samuel Ellis, wireless operator of the Australo-Canadian Shipping Company, am alone on the sinking forepart. I saw a wave carry off the raft on which were the rest of the crew of the *Timor.* The Chattertooths were aft, where Father Chattertooth had carried his luggage. These heroes seem to have gone mad. By the flashes of lightning I could see that they were unpacking their bags. All have now vanished. I am alone. The water is coming in under the door. The end is at hand. Our Father..."

The wireless operator of the *Argo* rose and stared at the strip of paper in which his apparatus had printed dots and dashes. He waited in vain: there was nothing more.

In a low whisper he finished the prayer for his colleague Samuel Ellis....

At five in the morning the *Argo* reached the tenth latitude off Manahaki Island. The sea was as smooth as the sky above it. Boats were lowered to collect the members of the crew of the *Timor* who were still clinging to the wreckage of the rafts. They were weak and stiff with cold, semi-conscious, but saved. At six in the morning, beyond the Manahaki reef they discovered a floating board, the remains of a door, to which the operator Ellis was desperately clinging. The *Argo* raised her anchor and cruised around. Every glass on board swept the green flood, and every scrap of wreckage was examined. By ten o'clock they had rescued the entire crew of the *Timor* from Captain Sweet to the youngest ship's boy.

The last find was made at half-past ten. The only boat that was still in the water by this time knocked against a small object as it was returning. Mr. Scrooge, who was giving a hand, leant over the side and fished up an old football.

The Chattertooths had vanished without trace, and the *Argo* steamed off with the passengers and both crews plunged in gloom.

XVII.   "To the deuce with this confounded heaving ocean. If I am not mistaken the game is over!"

"Father, father, you promised only yesterday evening that you would never swear again."

"The deuce! On my soul, I will never let another wretched swearword cross my lips!"

This conversation was carried on at five in the morning on the surface of the Pacific Ocean. None of those taking part in it knew the exact location, for the frightful storm had driven them for five hours through never-ending darkness. But now unexpectedly the power of the storm was suddenly broken, and as the sun came up in all its glory above the horizon the sea was calm once more, and innocent little waves splashed beneath the morning breeze and the clear sky was flushed with all the colours of the opal. In the midst of this splendour, which was mirrored in the blue-green waters with their crowns of white foam, twelve dark spots were floating. It was the famous Chattertooth team, the world champions, with old Father Chattertooth in the midst of them. They were all alive and sound and unhurt, and seemed to have escaped the fury of the waters by a miracle.

Was it a miracle? Yes, it was a miracle, but Father Chattertooth had had his finger in it. When he saw that the *Timor* could not hold together and that the hastily constructed rafts did not offer much safety, he ran down to his cabin and with Honza's help dragged on deck the vast trunk, famous by now, that he carried from match to match; the con-

tents the Chattertooths had used only once, in their historic encounter with the toughs of Barcelona. He brought out the twelve rubber suits, which were quite watertight. Eleven had been for his sons, the twelfth for their reserve man, which role he himself now played. By the flashes of the lightning they had slipped into these suits, twelve pumps had been busily wielded, and lo and behold, the stately forms of the Chattertooths had been transformed into twelve balloons from which only heads, arms and legs protruded. But their arms and legs, too, were protected with watertight rubber coverings, so that only their heads were exposed to the wind and the waves. They had quickly slipped food into their watertight kitbags, and when a huge wave had broken over the ship they launched their raft upon it. Hardly had they pushed off from the ship when a frightful groaning set them all shuddering. The side of the ship had been stove in, and the wreck of the *Timor* sank. With a wild soughing the waves rolled in over the hulk of the ship, but by this, time the raft of the Chattertooths was far enough away not to be sucked under. Now it became the plaything of the raging wind, which drove it on like a cork at unimaginable speed. The Chattertooths had to use all their strength to keep a hold on the raft as they clung there close together. After two hours of plunging forward, the raft vanished under them in the darkness, and the Chattertooths found themselves in the water. But the rubber of their dresses held, and they bobbed in the water like twelve strange buoys, driven on by the gusts of wind. They could not make their voices heard above the roar of the thunder and the waves, but that did not matter, for they held on tight to each other, possessed by the instinct not to let anything get the better of them, and built one solid body that refused to sink.

Now for the first time, as the fury of the storm subsided and the sun came up, they could relax for a moment and draw breath. They looked around, full of gratitude and trust in the Providence that had led them through this danger. In the glancing light and colours of the morning they saw themselves utterly alone in the expanse of splendour. Not a ship in sight, not a sign of land. This sobered them a little, but in their unbroken faith they did not lose their heads and the younger ones even began to enquire about breakfast. Father Chattertooth had nothing against the proposal that the kitbag containing biscuits and dried meat should be opened, and they tucked into it as though they had been picnicking in a glade in the woods of Nether Buckwheat.

Only Honza did not give his undivided attention to breakfast, but kept turning south-west. At last Father Chattertooth noticed it.

"De...," he nearly burst into his favourite oath, but then remembered his vow of the night before, swallowed back half of it and continued:

"What's up, Honza? What do you keep looking at?"

"I don't want to raise false hopes, but I wouldn't mind betting, Father, that there is an island over there, in the direction the wind and waves are carrying us."

"Where, where?" they cried, their eyes almost starting out of their heads as they stared in the direction he indicated.

The whole sky was still aflame with the violet, red and orange light of the sunrise. And in a nest of golden clouds, mist and haze, they caught a glimpse of something on the horizon which seemed to develop an ever sharper outline as they stared and stared.

"That's an island for sure, Honza."

They kept on staring with all their eyes into the far distance, where two peaks and a chain of mountains were clearly taking shape.

"An island, and the wind is carrying us there!"

For sheer joy the Chattertooths began playing in the water like seals. They would gladly have started a rough-and-tumble, but they were hindered by the melon-like suits they were wearing. So they only splashed about and shouted until someone finally asked how long it would take them to swim to the island.

"Wait a moment, boys," old Chattertooth broke in, "I have something. Hand your kitbag across, Frantik."

Frantik did as he was told, and his father took out a collapsible wooden framework and a vast

piece of canvas. Before the surprised boys could gather what he was about, he had unrolled the canvas and fastened each end of it to the wooden sticks. It was a long banner with the inscription:

THE CHATTERTOOTH ELEVEN

which the old man carried with him to head the triumphal processions of welcome in which his team was always taken from the station to their hotel. That was the only piece of showing off that old Chattertooth had ever allowed himself, and it had given him a childish pleasure. Now this banner had become an important item in the business of rescuing the Chattertooths.

The boys had grasped the idea at once, and broke out into shouts of joy. Here they had a sail: it was enough to unfurl it, and those who held it were blown forward by the wind at a lively pace and could pull the others behind them. It was clear, however, at the first attempt, that it was not so easy to carry the idea out, but the Chattertooths soon hit upon how it should be done: six of them had to form a wedge between the two poles so that the wind did not blow the whole thing over, and after that it was plain sailing. Naturally they had to take it in turns to carry the poles for it was hard work, and soon numbed their hands.

They had scarcely hit upon this idea before the wind was bowling them along at such a smart pace that the remaining four boys had scarcely time to grip those who were lined up with the sail. Thus they went forward at a fair speed south-westwards along the foaming crests of the waves. But the island was further off than they had supposed. Hour after hour went by and still it was only a grey shadow on the edge of the far horizon, little larger and clearer than it had been at first. At eleven o'clock the wind fell and the improvised sail drooped slackly down. Now they had to swim, and this was by no means pleasant in the oppressive heat which had prevailed since nine in the morning. But the boys swam, for therein lay their hope of rescue.

At four o'clock the wind sprang up again. They raised their sail once more and let the wind drive them onwards. By six o'clock they could already pick out the crinkly crowns of the palm trees on the green slopes and the white line of the surf breaking along the beach. As the sun went down they drew in their sail, for the wind had veered round and there was the danger that they might be blown past the island.

The Chattertooth banner vanished from the surface of the Pacific Ocean, but as the Southern Cross swung up the darkening sky the Chattertooth Eleven with old Father Chattertooth at their head crawled on to the beach after twenty hours in the water. They knelt down in silent prayer.

Now for the first time they were conscious of the peril they had escaped. They were like that. As long as danger hovered, they knew neither fear nor doubt. If there were obstacles, they had to be overcome. They never lost faith or hope, never sat with idle hands. Their whole education had taught them to fight the enemy and to face him with a clear head. They knew that to be happy and to do one's duty cheerfully were half the battle, and in the midst of the greatest danger it never occurred to them that things could end badly for them. But now that the danger was over, they realised what had been at stake. They were overcome with a feeling of boundless sweet gratitude: they would once again see Nether Buckwheat, their mother, the cottage by the woods, the eleven little white houses round the field, old Nero and the eleven happy girls who were awaiting their return. Their feeling of thankfulness was mixed with a feeling of exhaustion which descended suddenly upon them and overwhelmed them. They did not even want to eat. They laid aside their rubber suits, stretched themselves out under the palm trees, and in thirty seconds were asleep. They had not even thought about posting a sentry.

But a terrible yelling and howling aroused them from the depth of their sleep. They tried to spring up but they could not. Each of them was gripped by five, six, eight hideous savages, strangely tattoed, who bound them hand and foot to an accompaniment of wild cries.

The Chattertooths at once guessed what had happened. They had sought refuge on a cannibal island, and, scarcely escaped from one death, they now found themselves face to face with a second and far more terrible one.

XVIII.   Big Chief Birimarataoa had spiral decorations cut into the skin of his whole face. The lobes of his ears has been stretched to an unnatural length so that when the lower edge of one of them was folded up to the top edge and held fast with a pin, it made quite a decent sized pocket. In his right ear Birimarataoa carried a silver box containing snuff, and in the left a bunch of keys for a cashbox that could not be unlocked, a costly memorial of an American merchant. The most valuable ornament, however, was in Biramarataoa's nose, a yellow 3-B Koh-i-noor pencil.

Big Chief Birimarataoa sat on his throne surrounded by a circle of pedestalled gods with mouths agape. Three rows of savage warriors saw that none of the twelve Chattertooths attempted to escape as they stood before Birimarataoa.

Big Chief Birimarataoa with the wrinkled face and the blazing eyes ended the examination of the prisoners. A hideous old man with a necklace of teeth and claws was the interpreter.

"Great Birimarataoa," he said, bowing deeply, "know white man good. Hear say in island, brothers make good kick. Birimarataoa like kick. Who good kick make good fight. Great Birimarataoa have field, great Birimarataoa have team, Birimarataoa team make kick, white brothers make kick. If white brothers no good kick, Birimarataoa's team eat him. If white brothers better kick, great Birimarataoa make him go live. Birimarataoa very Big Chief."

"Your cannibalistic Majesty, Mr. King," said Mr. Chattertooth, whose speech was then translated into English by Honza, so that the loathsome old man could then turn it into Papuan, "if I am not mistaken, something like a match is the subject of discussion?"

"Yes, white brother make kick, team Birimarataoa make kick. Birimarataoa Big Chief."

"And when is this match to be?"

"Birimarataoa make tom-tom call people tomorrow afternoon. People love looksee kick. When kick make end, people make feast-eat. Birimarataoa Big Chief."

"May we have our kit for the match? We are accustomed to playing in dress."

"White brother get have all he want. Birimarataoa Big Chief."

"What sort of a ball have you?"

"Ball? What ball mean?"

"The ball, the round thing to kick."

"Ball? Make kick ball? Team Birimarataoa no make kick ball. Team Birimarataoa make kick white brother. Birimarataoa Big Chief."

Now it was Chattertooth's turn to be bewildered.

"What does that mean; kick brother?"

"So, make kick foot, make kick stomach, make kick nose, make kick all. But no make catch, no make hold, no make choke, no make with hands. That bad foul. And who make curse, he make lose. Birimatataoa Big Chief."

Father Chattertooth's face grew longer and longer. He opened his eyes wide and scratched himself behind the ear. But Big Chief Birimarataoa took his snuffbox from his right ear, took a pinch and sneezed: then he took the keys from his left ear and jingled them. This meant that the audience was at an end, and the warriors led the Chatter-tooths away to their hut.

As soon as they were alone old Chattertooth began to tear his hair and to lament bitterly.

"O my singed scalp, O my half-baked brain, you have done it, you have brought things to this pass! Fool, idiot, goose, donkey, that I am! What have I got in my head that I have never thought of such a thing. Now I have landed you all in a pretty kettle of fish. O my giddy football, now I've made a fine hash of things. Fool, idiot, goat, goose, donkey that I am!"

His eleven sons listened open-mouthed to the raving of the old man. At last Honza pulled himself together.

"But father, what is the matter? What are you so frightened of?"

"What am I frightened of?" the old man hissed. "You ask that? I am frightened of tomorrow, boy. What can you lads do against rough play? Goodness, you play as if you had kid gloves on your feet. And I have to let you loose against eleven cannibals without a ball. Don't you understand what it is all about? Why, tomorrow they will kick the stuffing out of you and make mincemeat of you. And you are supposed to try and do the same to them. Honza, you are the oldest and the strongest... Can you imagine yourself kicking anyone? Calmly measuring the distance and giving him a kick in the wind?"

"Good Heavens, father, I don't know, but I can sooner imagine myself not doing it than doing it."

"Naturally. That's just how I have trained you. You play like girls at a dancing academy, like cherubs, like chaperones. Your legs are a good deal better bred and politer than most people's mouths. Blockhead that I am. And now the fine football I've taught you will land you in the soup. Oh goodness! if only once a penalty kick had been given against us I might have some faint hope. But as it is, what can you in your innocence do against cannibals?"

He stopped in the middle of the hut and turned anxiously to his sons, his eyes troubled.

"Listen, boys. The best of fathers may be deceived in his children. I beg you, I beseech you, confess. Isn't one of you by any chance a bit spiteful? I may have thought that you were playing a clean, decent game, but perhaps one of you has given his opponent a sly kick now and again when no one was looking. I beg you, children, best of sons, isn't one of you a rough player? Think it over and make a clean breast of it. It would be such a joy to me."

The boys stood there, looked at one another, looked at the ground, and then looked at their father, and one after another they shook their heads. Chattertooth wrung his hands in despair.

"So we are up to our ears in the soup! Or rather in the frying-pan, like Christmas turkeys. I can already see my left side nicely roasted. I shall begin swearing soon, the deuce take it. A fine end for the world champions. Eaten up skin and bone."

He fell silent and looked sadly through the opening of the hut. He saw three more huts, and beyond them a large meadow. Obviously the sportsground where their fate would be decided tomorrow.

"Listen, father," said Jura. "We will find some trick or other to get us out of this mess. It's a difficult thing for us to kick other people, even if they are cannibals. But when you taught us how to avoid being tripped up and what to be on our guard against, there were one or two things that wouldn't come in at all badly now. I can't remember exactly how it was, but once in Berlin I got such a kick that I thought I should never be able to get up again. The centre-half laid me out without my even noticing that he had put a foot near me."

The longer he spoke, the more attentively old Chattertooth listened. He suddenly began to scratch himself: his whole body itched. His eyes began to shine, and soon he broke in on Jura.

"Stop, Jura! There's something in what you say. It is not only a question of kicking. Obviously! It's possible to get in a lot of high-class dirty work in the slickest way. What an old goat I was not to think of it sooner. Jura, good lad, give me a kiss. It's a brainwave. We will even give the cannibals a good hiding. You see how people can lose their heads. As if I had never seen a rough house at the pub! But now we must get to work quickly and stop talking. We've something new to learn."

Like a man reborn he took off his jacket, rolled up his shirtsleeves, and began to teach the boys all the forbidden tricks. The whole gamut, from a simple kick to knocking out an opponent, was practised. Father Chattertooth was aflame with eagerness, and the boys devoured his teaching with ear and eye.

"If you are walking or running slowly and your opponent does not move aside, you can do a fine bit of dirty work with your heel. Look here. The right foot is moving forwards, and now he takes a step. But instead of raising your left leg, raise your right heel. He is just on his toes, and he is just turning his right foot so that his heel turns outward. You have fallen one step behind him, but he is still moving in the same tempo. So he has just raised his left foot and is putting it forward. But instead of his coming down on it, he trips over your heel and goes sprawling..."

"And here's a neat way of knocking someone down from behind.

The boy is running in front of you and you are close behind him. Watch his feet. Now he has the left one behind him. Now he has raised it, the foot is in the air, but still behind him. At that moment kick him with your toes from outside on the ankle or the heel. Either will do. Better still, kick his toes. The raised leg is powerless in a person off his guard. Under your kick his leg is moved a couple of inches to the right. At this moment he is just ending his movement forward, but he is already thrown slightly out. And so his foot, instead of touching the ground, kicks the shinbone of his other leg. Down he goes, but to his dying day he won't be able to explain what happened to him."

Throughout the evening and far into the night there was a sound of trampling and falling, of quick commands and quiet talking, in the prison hut. At midnight Father Chattertooth finished his training.

"Cheating is cheating and the world's a dirty place," he said, mopping the sweat from his face. "But with God's help we shall escape the frying-pan."

XIX.   In the morning Father Chattertooth kept looking impatiently towards the village. He was waiting for the things that the cannibals had taken from them and which Big Chief Birimarataoa regarded as lawful prize. Father Chattertooth set great store on having them, especially the rubber suits. If they had kept the Spaniards at bay with them, it would be jolly bad luck if they couldn't manage the cannibals too. At midday a smile of joy at last spread over Father Chattertooth's face. In the village square there appeared the old interpreter and with him a crowd of tattoed monsters carrying the Chattertooth's things. Big Chief Birimarataoa had kept his word, for he thought that it would only be an hour or two before the fine things were back in his hands. So the Chattertooths had everything, their costumes, the pumps, and the kitbags full of food, for the savages had not been able to undo the zip fasteners. After lunch they began to blow each other up until they stood there like twelve vast footballs.

Meanwhile from outside there came the sound of the crowd crying and howling: wild singing, the beating of drums and trumpetings on the horns of animals were heard. Through the chinks in the walls of their straw hut the Chattertooths saw that masses of cannibals were taking up their stand all round the meadow. Their naked bodies, painted, tattooed and decorated with scars, shone in the sun as though rubbed with oil. Among them was raised a throne on which Big Chief Birimarataoa sat. From time to time he took a pinch of snuff from his box, which he always stowed away carefully in his ear

again. In the middle of the meadow eleven warriors were dancing their challenge to combat. They looked fearful, for they had drawn vast masks over their heads, hideous, terrifying diabolical faces meant to frighten not only their opponents but also the audience. Twenty priests beat drums and blew trumpets in time to the dance, while the cannibals howled and beat applause on their stomachs with their hands.

At last the dance was finished and the old interpreter bowed before the chief. With great dignity Birimarataoa unpinned his left ear, took out his keys and jingled them. The old man bowed and strode towards the Chattertooth's hut. The crowd had been pushed back and a funnel-shaped space cleared, at the broad end of which stood the eleven masked warriors. At the narrow end was the Chattertooth prison.

Suddenly the air was rent with blood-curdling howls. But these were not howls of hate, nor a warcry, but rather sounds of despair and fear. For from the hut came not the twelve victims earmarked for the feast that night, but eleven unknown gods, perfect in their huge rotundity, solemn in their slow walk, magnificent in every movement.

Thousands of hands were raised, with fingers outspread in supplication, as if to ward them off. In all their lives the people of Birimarataoa had never seen anything so sublime and superhuman, for though their priests were up to quite a number of dodges, they had never been able to create such globular forms. Hence the pearls cast up by the sea were held sacred by them.

And now they saw eleven living globes that seemed like celestial beings come to fight against the demons of the earth. All grew silent with awe, and only the priests were able to master their disquiet. They could not fail to notice that even the warriors were quaking behind their masks.

Big Chief Birimarataoa jingled his keys. The priests uttered a series of yells. The warriors answered them. And then they charged wildly across the meadow and made one huge, powerful kick at their globular opponents. The globes hardly stirred under the impact, and the cannibals bounced back. Once more they charged and once more kicked.

Once again they rebounded from the globes. Several of the warriors fell over, and others lost their masks, revealing faces twisted with terror. The priests began to howl and beat their drums, but the warriors were too afraid. They hung back and waited to see what the globes would do.

For a second everyone stood motionless, and then suddenly the spheres charged. With a speed such as none there had ever seen before they raced forward and threw themselves upon the black men. The impact was so great that the savages fell to the ground screaming with fear. But the globes remained standing and waited. The priests tried to encourage the warriors with cries and spurred them on to a fresh attack. Hesitatingly they began to move forward and the globes ran to meet them. But there was no further clash, for half-way the savages began to waver and then scattered in all directions. The globes set about them. Never has there been such confusion as followed. The savages stumbled, fell down, rolled on the ground, their noses and knees bleeding, squealed and jabbered, lost their masks and their necklaces of animals' teeth, stood up, knocked into each other and fell again. They were all filled with such terror that even Big Chief Birimarataoa himself drew his pencil out of his nose and began to chew the end.

Fifteen minutes from the start, the black warriors broke in panic through the circle of spectators and fled to the woods. The crowd fled behind them with crazy yells.

"Your cannibalistic Highness, Mr. King," said old Chattertooth, who suddenly popped up before the throne at this moment, "if I am not mistaken we are left alone on the field. And I think that he who makes stay, he make win."

"Yes," answered Birimarataoa through the mouth of the interpreter. "White brother make win, white brother make feast-banquet of Birimarataoa's people. In one minute make beginning feast-banquet. Birimarataoa Big Chief."

Father Chattertooth scratched himself behind his ear in perplexity.

"Your cannibalistic Highness, Mr. King, please don't be offended, but I should like to know what we shall have for supper."

"Hm, Birimarataoa make give great feast-banquet. White brother make sit with Birimarataoa. Birimarataoa make him joy. Birimarataoa Big Chief."

"Naturally, but I should very much like to know what we shall get to eat."

"What we make get eat? Centre-forward roast on skewer. Birimarataoa Big Chief."

Father Chattertooth blinked hard three times, his sons grew a little pale. But their father continued the conversation.

"Your cannibalistic Highness, I have a little request to make to you. We have fought according to your custom. Let us celebrate the victory according to our custom – with a victory race. We will wait for it till your folk come back."

Big Chief Birimarataoa gave his assent with a nod. From the woods came a far sound of wild shouting. Birimarataoa's people were chasing the defeated warriors. The Chattertooths thought with a start of why the hunt was taking place. While the black public drifted slowly back, Father Chattertooth bent across to Honza.

"When you left the hut," he whispered without attracting any attention, "I carried all our things to the lonely palm over there beyond the village. We must make our victory run in that direction. We will run in three rows, with you in the first one. Once you are clear of the village, race on ahead and gather up all our things. I think we shall screen you, and the savages won't see what is going on. We shall go slowly to the edge of the wood, but then instead of turning back we shall strike at top speed into the wood. You understand?"

Honza had understood, and he explained to the others.

Most of the people were back by now. Father Chattertooth begged for permission for the victory race to begin.

Birimarataoa jingled his keys. The boys fell into place beside their father, and singing the chorus of their anthem they set off at a comfortable trot.

Once beyond the last hut, Honza ran on ahead. The others caught him up at the palm tree. He had the kitbags of food slung across him. The Chattertooths went on at their easy jogtrot. But at the first tree of the wood they broke into their quickest sprint.

"Left to the brook and along it to the coast. Like a hundred yard race, you wretched team!"

Confused sounds reached them from the distance. They hurried through the grove and raced down the valley. From here they had been carried off by the cannibals the day before, trussed up like parcels. The sea could not be far away. The sweat was pouring down them, but they put up the best speed of their lives. The valley suddenly turned and the road dropped steeply. Between the trees they could see the shining surface of the sea. They could hear it lapping sleepily below them. They jumped rather than ran. At last they were down. With twenty leaps they crossed the brook. In its mouth lay twelve canoes of hollowed tree trunks. One of them was slender, light, and unusually long.

Honza sprang in and threw down the bags.

"Take the paddles from the rest of the canoes," cried Jura, and his brothers understood at once. In the meantime Honza and his father had dragged Birimarataoa's canoe into the water. The youngsters, their arms full of paddles, were beside them in a second. From the cliffs above came a cry of rage. Three arrows whizzed past them into the water. But the Chattertooths were already paddling hard and the canoe flew through the surf.

The shouting behind them on the slope grew louder, the rain of arrows thicker.

But the canoe sped on.

Then the Chattertooths saw that the first warriors had reached the water's edge and were hastening to the canoes. A new cry arose when they found the paddles missing.

But nevertheless they pushed out into the water, using then-hands as paddles. They were going fairly quickly, but they could not catch the Chattertooths with their twelve paddles. And so one of the savages, a tall slim fellow, stood up on the bows, swinging in his right hand a heavy, frightful spear.

"Look out!" cried old Chattertooth, and the boys turned. The spear flew through the air, shining like lightning and sped towards the Chattertooth canoe.

"One, two!" roared their father, and the boys bent to; their paddles with redoubled keenness.

The spear crashed into the side of the canoe and a sound of splintering wood was heard. A large piece broke off and the water came pouring in through the hole.

"We'll manage to caulk this leak somehow or other, but unless I am mistaken we saw a world-record in spear-throwing today."

And he was right, for none of the other spears reached the canoe, which flew on, although water came pouring in.

XX.   "And I say, Sparsit, that they are seals!"

"I assure you, Carlsson, that they are porpoises!"

"Want to bet on it?"

"Good!"

"Two quid, Sparsit !"

"Two quid, Carlsson!"

Mr. Sparsit and Mr. Carlsson shook hands on it, and then once more turned their glasses on those perplexing spots on the horizon. The rest of the passengers of the *Jellicoe* joined them, and the dispute soon spread.

In the meantime, gently rolling, the *Jellicoe* continued its way across the Pacific Ocean. The strange black spots that Mr. Sparsit had sighted after lunch had not moved from the spot and did not reveal themselves even to the best glass as anything more than mysterious round floating objects. There was a third opinion among the passengers, that this was a collection of buoys that had broken anchor during some storm or other and carried to this out-of-the-way corner of the earth. But a careful survey of the buoys had revealed that they kept changing their relative positions so rapidly and irregularly that only living creatures could come in question, and so they were either seals or porpoises at play.

Even the crew of the ship were interested in the problem, and for two hours they talked about firing some shots among the seals. Captain Fardy smilingly granted the request of his passengers and changed the course of the vessel by a couple of points to the north-west.

From five o'clock onward everybody on board was seized with a wild excitement, for the glasses had revealed that the twelve black points were twelve inordinately fat people.

What tragedy had happened here? And by what miracle had they been able to keep afloat? And what grim jest of fate had collected this apostolic number of fat men at this point?

Nobody could answer, and the imaginations of the passengers were as much under way as was the *Jellicoe* itself.

Shortly after six o'clock in the evening the lifeboats were lowered. In one of them sat Mr. Sparsit, in another Mr. Carlsson. Neither won his bet, but they wanted nevertheless to be the first to solve the riddle which they had been the first to discover.

The solution caused great astonishment, for as the boats came nearer they found, there in the midst of the Pacific Ocean, the world-famous Chattertooth Eleven. And in order not to get out of practice they were playing waterpolo with their father.

And this brings to an end the history of the Chattertooth Eleven.

A Tale of a Czech Football Team
for Boys Old and Young

THE CHATTERTOOTH ELEVEN
EDUARD BASS

English translation by Ruby Hobling
Illustrations by Jiří Grus
Foreword by Mark Corner
Layout by Zdeněk Ziegler

Published by Charles University
in Prague, Karolinum Press
Ovocný trh 3-5, 116 36 Prague 1
http://cupress.cuni.cz
Prague 2009
Vice-rector-editor
Prof. PhDr. Mojmír Horyna
Edited by Martin Janeček
Typeset by MU studio
Printed by PBtisk Příbram
Second English edition,
first by Karolinum Press

ISBN 978-80-246-1573-8